I0713732

MARILYN'S DRESS

GRAEME FRIEDMAN

Copyright © Graeme Friedman 2024

All rights reserved. The author asserts his moral rights in this work through the world without waiver. No part of this book may be reproduced, or stored in a retrieval system, or transmitted in any form or by any means, electronic, mechanical, photocopying, recording or otherwise without express written permission of the publisher.

All the characters depicted in the stories published in this book are fictitious, and any resemblance to actual persons, living or dead, is purely coincidental.

Published by Joanne Fedler Media 2024
www.joannefedler.com

ISBN: 978-1-925842-50-0 Paperback
ISBN: 978-1-925842-51-7 Ebook

Internal design by Ida Jansson

Cover design by Zeppelin Design

*The author and Joanne Fedler
Media acknowledge and honour
that this book was published on
the land of the First Nations of
Australia. We pay our respects to
their Elders past and present.*

By the same author

NOVELS

The Fossil Artist

What the Boy Hears When the Girl Dreams

NON-FICTION

The Piano War

Madiba's Boys: the Stories of
Lucas Radebe and Mark Fish
(with a foreword by Nelson Mandela)

Leaning Into Love: the Secrets to Finding
and Keeping Intimacy
(co-authored with Joanne Fedler)

EDITED ANTHOLOGY

A Writer in Stone: South African Writers
Celebrate the 70th Birthday of Lionel Abrahams
(co-edited with Roy Blumenthal)

For Peta,
beloved sister

CONTENTS

Acknowledgements   I

Foreword   VII

Marilyn's Dress   1

Patrick's Deli   21

The Finger of God   35

A Spy in the House of Art   49

The Demobbing   71

Ripple Effect   91

The Beggar in the Bookshop   101

Fugue   119

Golem Heights   133

About the Author   169

Acknowledgements

These stories were written during the period 1996 to 2003. Reading them in preparation for this volume, with their archaic references to floppy drives and telephone landlines, they feel like time capsules. They also constitute a time capsule of my concerns: the legacies of apartheid, ongoing injustice, violence against women, personal loss, the hubris of human beings. I hope, dear reader, that the suffering I have depicted is balanced with empathy and humour, a dollop of schadenfreude, and the sort of liberation that leads to healing.

I was mentored as a writer by poet, novelist, and man of letters, Lionel Abrahams, who, as a young aspiring author, was tutored by Herman Charles Bosman, arguably South Africa's greatest short story writer. 'You have to write and write,' Bosman told

Lionel, '– ten years for the wastepaper basket.' I have been fortunate in that, largely due to Lionel and the members of his writers' workshop, my first ten years saw the publication of many of the stories gathered in this collection, as well as my first two non-fiction books. I owe a huge debt to the generosity and astute readership of that collective, as well as to the editors, publishers, and literary award judges who gave my stories recognition.

I thank Tim Conradie for recollections that inspired 'The Beggar in the Bookshop', and Leslie Sheills, the man with a magic flute, for giving me the language and understanding of a flautist's passion to write 'Fugue'. I hope I've done justice to both Tim's and Leslie's gifts.

'The Demobbing' is based on actual events that took place during the Messina Landmine Trial in which I participated as an expert psychology witness on behalf of the two accused African National Congress guerrillas. Some of the trial evidence is taken verbatim from the court record; however, the characters depicted in the story are entirely inventions of my imagination and do not resemble any actual individuals. Nevertheless, I acknowledge Judge Azhar Cachalia, Dr Lloyd Vogelman, and the late Rodney Black for their respective roles, as well as the sufferers of political violence on both sides of the horrific conflict that resulted in those tragic events.

I am profoundly indebted to my dear friend, co-writer, and now publisher, Joanne Fedler, without whom this collection, as well as other work of mine, would not be in readers' hands.

The contribution of a foreword by Isabel Balseiro, Professor of Comparative Literature at Harvey Mudd College, California, is a blessing for me on two levels: primarily for the insightful and graceful way in which she situates the stories of this volume, but also because of the publication history of the titular 'Marilyn's Dress', Isabel having included it in her edited anthology *Running Towards Us: New Writing from South Africa* (2000). I am delighted by, and deeply grateful for, the care she has taken.

And finally, I have lived my dream as a writer due to the generous encouragement and support of my wife and first reader, Tracey Segel, who suggested this short story collection and who, many years ago, after I had finished 'Marilyn's Dress', encouraged me to submit it to a writing competition run by a feminist literary journal. 'But it's for women,' I protested. 'No,' she corrected me, 'it's about women. Don't decide for them who is eligible.' I duly submitted the story, and it won. But the most treasured prize I ever won is the family, with our children Davey, Matt, and Asha, we have created together. Love, after all, is the best story.

The author and current publisher would like to thank the editors, translators, and publishers of the anthologies in which several of the short stories appearing in this collection have previously been published:

'Marilyn's Dress' in *Running Towards Us: New Writing from South Africa*, edited by Isabel Balseiro (Heinemann, 2000); and *herStoria* (Vol.2, No.3, Summer 1996);

'Patrick's Deli' in *Electronic Sesame III*, edited by Roy Blumenthal (Barefoot Press, 1998);

'The Finger of God' in *At the Rendezvous of Victory and Other Stories*, edited by Andries Oliphant (Kwela Books, 1999); *herStoria* (Vol.4, No.2, Winter 1998); *Sydafrika berättar: En stereo i Soweto*, Swedish translation by Jan Ristarp (Tranan, 2005); and *Svenska Impulser Noveller*, Swedish translation by Jan Ristarp (Sanoma, 2024);

'A Spy in the House of Art' in *Opbrud*, edited by Chris van Wyk, Danish translation by Finn Holten Hansen, Marianne Madelung & Helen Gaohenngwe

Seiketso (AKS/Hjulet, 2000); and *Post-Traumatic*, edited by Chris van Wyk (Botsotso Publishing, 2003);

'The Demobbing' in *Jewish Writing in the Contemporary World: South Africa*, edited by Claudia Braude (Nebraska University Press, 2001); and

'The Beggar in the Bookshop' in *A Writer in Stone*, edited by Graeme Friedman & Roy Blumenthal (David Philip, 1998).

Foreword

"Time is the substance I am made of. Time is a river which sweeps me along, but I am the river; it is a tiger which destroys me, but I am the tiger; it is a fire which consumes me, but I am the fire."

JORGE LUIS BORGES

(*Labyrinths: Selected Stories and other Writings*)

With the nine short stories included in *Marilyn's Dress*, Graeme Friedman takes us back to the dramatic changes South Africa experienced from 1996 to 2003, acknowledging that, "they also constitute a time capsule of my concerns: the legacies of apartheid, ongoing injustice, violence against women, personal loss, the hubris of human beings" (p.i). Prompting fresh ways of understanding South African cultural history, the collection moves beyond ideas based on difference into the tangled and complex forms of interdependence that marks democratic South Africa.

Situating the book in the context of post-1994 writing requires some mention of the historical backdrop then and now. The political transition in the Age of Mandela brought with it a liberatory exultation for most of the country's population. After more than three centuries of European domination, what Archbishop Desmond Tutu would dub "the Rainbow Nation," another optimistic symbol for the "New" South Africa, was filled with joy. Nelson Mandela, the "Father of the Nation," went from prisoner to president, the harbinger of a healthy kind of nationalism won after a tortuous journey from bondage to the voting polls. Other symbols of freedom, like the Constitution, the anthem, the flag, the Truth and Reconciliation Commission (TRC), civic restitution through Thabo Mbeki's call for an "African Renaissance," along with political, social, and economic institutional reforms, held the promise of national coexistence. Nonetheless, all these symbols, in conjunction with the neo-liberal global economy, have not been able to secure the incorporation of the previously marginalized majority into a unified whole. The shortcomings of the Rainbow

Nation are evident on several levels: restorative justice did not deliver the truth or compensation to countless survivors, the amnesty process favored too many perpetrators, and insufficient reparations were made to victims. Most disheartening, support for democracy seems to be declining as South Africa continues to be dominated by one party and, in recent years, one government after another has been dogged by a failure to deliver the changes the country deserved. Large numbers of students have scant access to quality education, African languages continue to take backstage to formerly colonial tongues, and the economy has bifurcated with Black technocrats in charge in the public sector while white financiers continue to run the private sphere. Significantly, the percentage of Black ownership and control in the private sector remains unsatisfactory while land reform has not yet secured tenure nor redistribution. This situation has generated a pervading sense of disappointment on many fronts. Then there is the corruption.

By 2024, when the seventh democratic general election is held, the African National Congress (ANC) will have been in power for close to three decades. Disillusion with the ANC is mixed with concern over the alternatives. Will a Democratic Alliance roll back some of the gains the earlier ANC government has given them? Is the Economic Freedom Fighters (EFF) too radical, reckless, and inexperienced to be trusted with maintaining a functioning and stable state? All too many South Africans may not even bother to vote anymore. The new South Africa has labored both to unravel a fraught past and to keep alive the aspirations of a diverse citizenry. The gains since liberation must be acknowledged – but the disenchantment is palpable. The current troubling uncertainties do not come out of the blue and warning signs have been registered by the literary chroniclers of a nation struggling hard with the demands of full democratization. Graeme Friedman's short stories need to be considered within this larger picture of post-Apartheid politics and literature.

A good number of the imaginative works reflecting the post-transition era have been marked by aporia. From the late K. Sello Duiker's *Thirteen Cents* (1999) and *The Quiet Violence of Dreams* (2001) as well as Phaswane Mpe's *Welcome to Our Hillbrow* (2001) to the turning point of J. M. Coetzee's *Disgrace* (1999). The novel's unsparing portrayal of gang rape, racial strife, and white male disempowerment stirred such a negative response that the ANC denounced what was interpreted as Coetzee's catastrophic vision of a post-Apartheid society. Other renditions of the Zeitgeist range from a sobering dissection of the Truth and Reconciliation Commission in Achmat Dangor's *Bitter Fruit* (2001) to the shift to transnational aesthetics ushered in by Ishtiyaq Shukri's *The Silent Minaret* (2005) and *I See You* (2015). There is also the granular focus on young Black male experiences of Niq Mhlongo's *Dog Eat Dog* (2004) and Kgebetli Moele's *Room 207* (2009). Women's contributions to a distinctly sour aftertaste in post-Apartheid literature include works like Kopano Matlwa's *Coconut* (2007) and *Spilt Milk* (2010), and Sindiwe Magona's *Beauty's Gift* (2008), as well as the original remaking of history through neo-slave narratives by Yvette Christiansë (*Unconfessed*, 2006) and Rayda Jacobs (*The Slave Books*, 1998). And, in sync with continental trends, one finds the Afropolitanism of émigré writers like Kagiso Lesego Molope or Zukiswa Wanner. Friedman's short fiction shares some of the disquiet and unease perceptible in these narratives, often from the perspective of an unusually insightful child or a questioning outsider.

"They moved so well in their own world," Josie realizes as the seals bob above and below the water's surface where she waits to meet the boat that will bring Uncle Albert. She is eight years old and besotted with her mother's beauty and the dream world conjured by the garment that gives title both to the opening short story and to this haunting collection. "Marilyn's Dress" describes a place, physical and psychic, in which animals seem at ease in their habitat in contrast to the humans around her. Margaret, Josie's mother, shaken by the violence unleashed on her by her husband just the night before, a husband complicit in Josie's molestation at the hands of her uncle, attempts an escape into the sea. The roughness of the ocean encircling the unnamed, if recognizable, island serves as a metaphor for the inner lives of these dysfunctional characters.

A penal colony since the times when the Dutch East India Company ruled the land, Robben Island is synonymous with exile and isolation. But it is also rich in flora and fauna (*robben* is Afrikaans for this mammal), like the seals that Josie observes frolicking in the waters. And it is these two sides of the isle, apparently irreconcilable, that coexist in "Marilyn's Dress." The institutional brutality for which Robben

Island became known is present through Brandt, Josie's father and Margaret's husband, a warder tasked with inflicting pain and suffering on inmates. But in crushing the morale of the prisoners, Brandt and the coworkers he drinks with themselves undergo a process of dehumanization that leaves them without empathy even for their own kin. Those imprisoned, on the other hand, find a measure of liberation by caring for one another. Indeed, in South Africa's fight against Apartheid, Robben Island stands as a symbol for overcoming adversity, which, in Margaret's case, is embodied in her unlikely escape and salvation of her daughters.

While the signs of a society riven by sexual and racial violence characterize the title story, the escape valve of cinema ("Patrick's Deli" and "Golem Heights"), the quagmire of memory ("The Finger of God" and "Ripple Effect"), the cyclicity of migration ("Fugue" and "Golem Heights"), and the shifting of identity ("A Spy in the House of Art," "The Demobbing" and "The Beggar in the Bookshop") abound in *Marilyn's Dress*. Stories like "The Demobbing," "Fugue" and "Golem Heights" (all tracing Jewish sediments on African soil) are stepping stones toward a socially and intellectually integrated cultural formation that affirms polyvocality and inclusion. Instead of focusing on ideas of embodiment and difference, this book pivots on the concept of race as a social category shaped by historical forces and unsuspected routings. These three tales explore the movement of the Jewish Diaspora from Eastern Europe to South Africa, from the nineteenth century onwards, and navigate issues of migration, hybridity, cultural hesitation, and a blurring of boundaries.

In "The Demobbing," for example, clinical psychologist Leonard Rosenthal, an expert witness for the defense in trials against uMkhonto we Sizwe (MK), the armed wing of the African National Congress, during the 1980s, encounters Kobus Venter in his practice, once the victim of an MK politically motivated attack. At one point in a cross-examination during the Apartheid years, the prosecutor had asked, "Rosenthal. That's Jewish isn´t it? Are you a Jew?" which leads the expert witness to reflect:

Of course, Rosenthal is a Jewish name but was I a Jew? I hadn't been inside a synagogue since a cousin's bar mitzvah years before. At the reception I had refused to stand for the singing of 'Die Stem' and had remained sitting when the band rolled its way into the first bars of 'Hatikvah'. It seemed to me we should not be standing for the national anthems of two oppressive states. I was not alone in these beliefs; the white left had a disproportionate number of Jews, and several leading communists were of Jewish ancestry. But the vast majority of South African Jews did not speak out; they were satisfied to keep their heads down, to stay in favour with the ruling party. Worse, many were like the devoutly Jewish Percy Yutar, prosecutor of the Rivonia Trial, trying desperately to prove that Jews were good patriots… Ironic. For an apartheid agent, being Jewish meant you are a communist traitor. For a left-wing Jew like me, it meant you are an apartheid collaborator (pp.82-84).

The story thus probes the ever-shifting perspectives in identity and, ultimately, the thin line of culpability. Upon Kobus Vester, who lost his wife and children in a landmine explosion, asking Rosenthal almost the same question decades later ("That's Jewish, isn't it?" p.82), Rosenthal wonders:

Was this to be another cross-examination? For seven years during South Africa's civil war, I went from courtroom to courtroom, fighting confessions and death penalties, laying accusations of apartheid horrors, of torture and assassination, of state-sponsored terror, in answer to the state's accusation of terror towards my comrades, the layer of landmines, the planter of bombs in shopping centres, the tyre-burning executioners of suspected collaborators. I turned my profession into a weapon, a storytelling weapon. I mounted the witness box, mounted my weapon, fired away with political narratives dressed up as psychological expertise, tried to duck for cover when the apartheid agents, the prosecutors and judges and magistrates, fired back. Was my weapon that indistinguishable from an AK-47 or a landmine? Was I not… a terrorist-supporting communist Jew, to be held partially accountable post-facto for the loss of Kobus Venter's wife and children? (pp.84-85)

The fact that this narrative is based on Graeme Friedman's experience both as a clinical psychologist and an anti-Apartheid activist, someone who gave evidence for liberation movement fighters, makes "The Demobbing" all the more gut-wrenching in terms of the tensions it builds between ethnicity, faith, political allegiance, place and one's positioning within such current debates as the memorialization of trauma and the ethics and aesthetics of truth and reconciliation. The anchor of an unforgiving past, indeed, creates gravitas and depth of loss throughout Friedman's prose. But perhaps the story that most vividly exemplifies his intricately dense narrative layering is the last.

The final piece in *Marilyn's Dress*, "Golem Heights," is set in the Johannesburg neighborhood of Hillbrow. In post-Apartheid's literary imagination, Hillbrow encapsulates all that's disturbing and hopeful about the new South Africa. While a scene of drugs, crime, and xenophobia toward immigrants from other African countries, Hillbrow is what some postcolonial theorists have taken to calling Afropolitan, a space that transcends national boundaries and suggests a Pan-African consciousness. The neighborhood may be in ruins, yet the taking over by Blacks, whether South African or not, of a once South African Jewish enclave clings to the promise that real transformation may yet still be possible. The story is also a modernist take on Yiddish literature through the figure alluded to in its title, the golem, a supernatural being brought to life, out of dust or clay, by incantations and the uttering of Hebrew letters to protect against virulent anti-Semitism. Likewise, "Golem Heights" takes inspiration from European art through poignant references to pre-WWII German silent cinema (*Der Golem, The Last Laugh, The Student of Prague*, etc.). The focal point is that of Miriam Gotkin, a Ph.D. student writing a thesis entitled "German Silent Cinema and the Treaty of Versailles: Art, Propaganda, and the Vengeance of the Fallen" (p.151). She wants to interview Herbert Neumann, one of the few remaining actors from the period, who lives in a building still recognizable from Miriam's childhood years:

> Like many buildings in the suburb, this one was art deco. But not for this place the Lebensraum-grab of closed-in balconies, the graffitied brickwork and grimy, blistered plaster, the washing hanging limp from windows. The building was ageing gracefully, the maintenance immaculate, the façade unadorned by the desperate overflow of people's lives. It was as if the place had forgotten to fall apart, a healthy member of a set of necrotic teeth. (p.138)

Only under the vigilant watch of its Czech doorman has the structure been spared the dilapidation of its surroundings. Is he the golem of the title, standing guard over the Jewish occupants? If so, that someone protects the art deco building, and its inhabitants, could well be a hint to the necessity of armed forces – signaled not just by the "Lebensraum-grab" quoted above but also the repeated mention of "Emperor Qin Shi Huang's terracotta soldiers" (p.158). Though, perhaps, another possibility is that the golem may be either Rabbi Herbert Neumann, a Doppelgänger of the doorman (also of Eastern European ancestry, about the same age, and who dies or disappears on the same day) or, symbolically, even the building itself. The openness of the text invites us to wonder. One layer of the narrative leaves scant doubt that something is crumbling and that protection against it and a yearning for peace will not be sustained by force alone. Then, Rabbi Neumann's young great-granddaughter (also named Miriam) is sick and dies of cancer, a disease that may be spreading into what an enigmatic character by the name of Mr. Nguni calls "*Indlu ka-Israyeli*" (p.145): the building no longer a haven for the survivors of the Shoah who sought shelter there. That is the reason why, by the story's conclusion, the Jewish population of Hillbrow flees to leafy suburbs where living behind electrified fences and armed guards outside awaits them – the cancer of insecurity metastasizing in post-A South Africa.

However one chooses to interpret the myth of the golem, an alternate reality is at play here – not unlike that present in the preceding story of emigration, the oneiric "Fugue." Given the isiZulu name adjudicated to the Hillbrow art deco building, House of Israel, a duplicity is invoked whereby Friedman, plunging into psychoanalysis, reminds us that there is a duality in groups involved in intergenerational trauma: the sufferer of oppression can, later, become the oppressor. The golem is an inanimate creature conjured to protect but when it becomes a threat, it must be destroyed. Birth and death, hope and threat, creation, salvation, but also power and control.

"Golem Heights" ends with a ghostly image. In the last paragraph of the book, after she learns that the rabbi and his great-granddaughter are dead, Miriam Gotkin notices: "At the foot of the black name board was a big chunk of the broken pot the cleaners must have missed. I stooped to look at it. What I thought was the rough inside of the piece, since it was so deeply furrowed, was convex, and in the dim light looked like a Greek bas-relief sculpture depicting the part of a face, the lips and scarred cheeks, the hollow of an eye socket and a fragment of the forehead, of the old Czech Doorman" (p.167).

Untethered from reality now, the short story morphs into magic realism or, rather, by its end the book arrives at what Jorge Luis Borges identifies as the confluence of narrative art and magic, a theory of fantastic literature he developed in an essay published in 1932. For the Argentine, imaginative or fantastic fiction is superior to other kinds because of its broader, "magical" notion of causality linking elements by similarity and contiguity as well as by logical cause and effect. Like the fragment of the shattered pot in "Golem Heights," golems are made of clay as are *sherblachs*, pottery shards placed on a dead person's eyelids symbolizing broken earth over a broken life. Rabbi Neumann is found lifeless on the ground, near scattered pieces of the pot it is assumed he must have fallen against in the entrance hallway to the building. The chunk of the broken pot with the effigy of the Czech Doorman is convex, as the lenses of cameras used in cinema – a leitmotif in the collection through which the author pays homage to the political use of the arts.

Perhaps the gift of the time capsules Graeme Friedman delivers in *Marilyn's Dress* lies in their capacity to transcend chronology.

XXII

Isabel Balseiro
Alexander and Adelaide Hixon Chair in the Humanities
and Professor of Comparative Literature,
Harvey Mudd College

Madrid, 14 October 2023

MARILYN'S DRESS

The girl peeks out from behind the rock as her mother walks toward the breakers. The small beach, sheltered from the settlement by the slope of the island's rocky terrain, faces across the strait. Somewhere to the hinterland are the neat rows of warders' homes that stand outside the walls of the prison. Today the mainland's harbour with its cargo ships, oil tankers, liners, and cranes, the coastal belt of luxury flats and hotels, the promenade that acts as a moat between the sea and the suburb, all lie hidden within the mist. Josie and her mother, Margaret, could be the only people on earth.

The hem of the girl's skirt is damp from kneeling on the wet sand. She frowns, noticing the water-darkened edges of the floral pattern, and knows what her mother will say.

'Josie!' she'll scold, 'you've gone and got your dress dirty. It's only just come back from the wash!'

'But Mom!'

'Listen to me now, my girl.' But there will be nothing more for Josie to listen to, her mother's thoughts will wander off, distracted.

Steadying herself against the cold rock surface, Josie rises from her knees. She brushes at the grains of sand that cling to her dress. Her blonde hair – some say it is almost white – is pulled back by an Alice band and falls just short of her shoulders. Her cheeks are flushed.

The tide is low, and her mother's feet make deep indentations in the wet, yielding sand... heel, ball, toe... heel, ball, toe... neither hurried nor slow, an unbroken rhythm of prints on their path into the sea.

It is a Saturday, the day for spring-cleaning. A few hours before, Margaret had started her work in the kitchen, on the stove which had served the families of correctional department servicemen since before the war, and rubbed away at the metal until Josie could see her face in it. Margaret had worked her way around the house, wiping, rubbing, dusting, sweeping, items touched, moved, picked up and attended to, always in the same order.

It was a small house with a corrugated iron roof. Last summer the peeling red paint was scraped off and the roof repainted by the prisoners. Josie had heard her parents discussing it.

'They're sweating like pigs up there,' Margaret had remarked.

There was a living room and two bedrooms, one for Josie and her little sister, Beth, and one for their parents. The family ate in the kitchen, around a wooden table. It was Josie's job to lay the table. All the warders' houses were not as small, but Josie's father, Brandt, was not senior enough to be allocated one of the bigger homes. They had only been on the island for eighteen months.

Josie was eight years old. She attended the little school that overlooked the parade ground. Her afternoons were spent playing outside with the children of the warders' families, helping about the house, or at other times, getting underfoot. That's what her mother called it. *Underfoot.*

'You're underfoot, Josie, go and entertain yourself,' Margaret would say.

'What are you making, Mom? Can't I help you?' Perhaps her mother would be sewing, the old black Singer's brass wheel with its thick, stubby spokes spinning round like those giant wheels at a fairground.

'You're underfoot, Josie.'

'I want to help you.' The needle of the Singer would whirr up and down, invisible to the naked eye, disappearing as if under a magician's spell. Until it would slow down, and Josie would catch sight of its secret mission: the needle piercing the material, and drawing the thread through, and back.

In recent months Margaret had taken to singing while she worked. It was always the same song, the same far-away voice, as if she'd just woken up but was still in a dream.

'Happy birthday, Mr President, happy birthday to you...'

Once she noticed Josie staring at her, and she said, 'I'm singing for the president, Josie, in America. I'm singing for President Kennedy.'

In the bedroom things were different between Josie and Margaret. There was more time for talk. The girl would lie on her tummy on the bed, her face propped up by her hands, her ankles crossing and re-crossing themselves. She would suck on the ends of her hair.

Looking at herself in the dressing table mirror, Margaret would toss her own hair.

'What do you think, Josie? Do you like it?'

'Yes! It looks wonderful, Mom.'

'Marilyn wore it this way, when she was alive.'

Josie would watch her mother dyeing her hair platinum blonde over the kitchen sink.

'You won't need to do this, not like Marilyn and me.'

Those were their best times together, Josie hanging about the long, beautiful legs of her mother.

'Happy birthday, Mr President, happy birthday to you...'

Margaret, singing for the great man across the sea. President Kennedy was also dead.

There were no friends for Josie's mother on the island. The warders' wives were mostly older than her or, Margaret would say, 'From the other side of the tracks. They don't like us because I'm English.' When Brandt was at work, she played The Beatles and Little Richard on the record player, and the wives didn't like that either.

Josie's best friend was Annetjie, the Colonel's granddaughter who came to stay on the island, along with her mother and four siblings. Her father had been killed in a mining accident. He was the only white man amongst forty-five men who were in a lift when the cable snapped. It took a week before the bodies could be recovered. People said what a shame he had to die in that way.

The girls played hide-and-seek in the lepers' graveyard, and hopscotch on the parade ground when the men weren't using it. Sometimes they played with the boys and once, after they dared her – four boys ranging in age from five to eleven, their hands on their hips, crew-cut heads jaunty in expectant triumph – Josie shimmied up the flagpole until she could touch the flag.

Best of all she enjoyed her private conversations with Annetjie behind the rows of haphazard, overgrown piles of rocks that stood for gravestones in the lepers' cemetery. A few weeks before they had been there, on the other side of the island, between the old graves and the sea, where the land slopes gently, then falls sharply away into the rumble of water. Josie had a stick in her hand, and pointed to the north-west, where they could see only the horizon.

'Look, you can see forever.'

'Tell me about the pirates,' said Annetjie.

'See there,' Josie said. 'There's an old pirate whose

name is Blackbeard. He's coming from far away across the ocean to fetch us. He'll bring his ship offshore and row his skiff to the beach and take us away with him to find treasure.' She dug in the burnt sand with the stick. 'He's the president of his country... we'll take prisoners along to row and President Blackbeard'll give us turns to whip them.'

A large oil tanker sailed slowly past. They had been coming more frequently because of the troubles in the Holy Land.

'Josie, do you think we'd be able to swim out to President Blackbeard's ship?'

'Sure.' Josie shaded her eyes, scanning the ocean. They were quiet for a few minutes. From the quarry came sounds of the men digging. Josie scratched the lines of a boat in the earth. 'My Dad says kaffirs can't swim, that's why they put them here. My Dad's a good swimmer, he was champion when he was in the navy. Mom can't swim, she hates the water.' Margaret had been pushed into a swimming pool when she was a little girl. 'My Dad tells me stories about Alcatraz and Devil's Island. He says all the best prisons are on islands, it's the natural place to keep dangerous men.'

Josie crouches behind the rock, watching the water swirl around her mother's well-formed dancer's calves. Her dress has again become trapped between her knee and the wet sand. She sucks at the ends of her hair, the faint taste of Sunlight soap on her tongue. She watches her mother intently. The sea makes way for Margaret, the white water froths around her shins, splashes up against her knees and thighs...

Sundays on the island were different. Sundays brought with them the approval of her father. Brandt liked it when Josie put on her church dress and Margaret helped do her hair into one long plait. This, he said, was her golden ponytail. She was a unicorn, and she wore her horn at the back of her head.

Sunday after Sunday, Brandt would tell Margaret, 'I'm just going for a beer, Margie. I'll catch up with you at church.' The rest of the week he called her Margaret. 'Come on, champ,' he'd call to Josie. And they'd walk hand-in-hand to one of the other warder's homes where the men would sit around on the small back porch looking at the orange earth, sipping from their beer glasses, talking about rugby, about handguns and rifles, and about women. That dress of Josie's, made on her mother's Singer, had lace cuffs and a lace collar and a mauve satin ribbon at the neck.

'Brandt, she's looking so pretty, hey!' someone would say as they passed her from one lap to another.

'Have a sip, skat. Hey, you don't mind do you Brandt?'

'Nee, wat...'

Josie would screw up her face. 'Ugh! It tastes awful!' And the men would laugh.

After a few drinks they'd forget about her. 'You go ahead, champ,' Brandt would say, after he'd noticed her hovering, her hands behind her back, trying not to move around in the dusty backyard in case she got her clothes and shoes dirty. 'I'll catch up with you.'

She'd look over her shoulder as she left the yard. Brandt, already oblivious of her, would be talking with the others. In the moments before Josie ran off to church to join her mother Margaret, her little sister Beth and God, her head would be filled with the sights and sounds of warders clinking beer bottles, scratching unshaven cheeks, bleary-eyed and comradely, each one drawn back into the circle of men.

Sometimes Brandt's brother Albert came to visit on the island. He'd been on the police force in Rhodesia but they'd kicked him out. Brandt would take Josie down to the quay to meet the boat. She'd listen out for the barks of the seals, and try to find their dark, blubbery forms under the water's surface. They moved so well in their own world.

Albert arrived on Friday night. Brandt had taken Josie to meet him. Later, well after she had gone to bed, she'd heard the men come home. They'd been at the pub, and Albert was shouting something about his boss at the factory where Brandt had found him a job. Josie had pretended to be asleep when they came into the room she shared with Beth.

'Ag, moenie worry nie, boet, there's room enough for the two of us, she's only little.'

'Okay, boet, sien jou môre,' Brandt had slurred before lurching off to bed.

It came back to Josie as she knelt behind the rock watching Margaret enter the sea, the sound of Uncle Albert taking off his clothes, the crumpled drop to the worn carpet, the movement of the sheets, the give of the mattress. He stank of fish and beer.

'Hello, Josie. It's me, Uncle Albert.' His beard had prickled against her neck, through her fine blonde hair.

Josie had kept quiet, breathing in a way she prayed

would sound like sleep.

'It's so cold outside, let's snuggle warm. Here, make your uncle warm.'

Dad was a champion swimmer... Mom hated the sea... Dad called her 'champ', he loved her church dress, the collar of lace... Blackbeard's gonna come from across the ocean... ag, moenie worry nie boet, there's room enough for the two of us... happy birthday, Mr President, happy birthday to you...

Beth had cried out, woken by Josie's muffled protests, and the cries had woken Margaret. There had been a great deal of shouting and screaming, the little girls' father telling their mother to calm down.

'You're hysterical, woman. Margaret, shut up! Calm down!' Then he'd hit her. With his fist. Against her eye. She fell and he took her by the hair and dragged her out of the room.

As Josie watches Margaret wade deeper into the sea, against the misty wand that has made the mainland disappear – perhaps forever – she can't stop herself from remembering, and from not remembering. Lying in her bed, yes, the covers over her head, her shivering knees tucked in beneath her chin, sucking on her Sunlight-washed hair, an acrid, awful sweetness pervading the dark space beneath the blankets.

And in the morning, she found Margaret cleaning the stove. Brandt was in his warder's trousers with his braces over his bare chest and shoulders, having breakfast with Uncle Albert and giving orders to Margaret about how they wanted their eggs. They were laughing about something. Margaret's hair was tied up in a doek. Her hands scrubbed faster and harder. When the brothers left the house Uncle Albert playfully slapped her bottom.

Margaret finished polishing the stove and the floors and went outside to do the stoep. After a while the red floor was so gleamy Josie could see her face in there too. She closed her eyes and tried to pretend that she could no longer see but the sights came through her ears. The soft scooping of the polish, the dull scraping of the tin on the stoep floor, her mother's panting for breath. She pushed her palms against her ears, tightly enough to hear the drone of the ocean. The little girl hung around waiting, hoping, for her mother to scold her for being underfoot.

When she was finished Margaret stood on the stoep for a long time with the tin of polish in one hand and her rags in the other, staring at the big palm tree in front of the house, her forehead wet with sweat, the rise and fall of her breasts gradually calming. People walked past, some greeted her. She stared at the palm tree.

Finally, she went into her bedroom and put on 'Marilyn's dress'. Before they'd come to the island, she'd taken Josie on the train to Stuttafords in town with money she saved from her housekeeping. They had tea at the posh restaurant. Margaret said the dressmaker's pattern and the material were precisely what she'd been looking for. She'd be able to make an outfit just like the one Marilyn wore in *The Seven Year Itch*, in the famous scene where her skirt billows up around her thighs.

Although she'd finished the dress before coming to the island, she'd not worn it before. It had a bodice that consisted of a halter-neck that gathered around the back of her neck, and from there descended frontwards, wrapping itself around each breast before being joined to the waistband and the pleated skirt below. Brandt had not allowed her to wear it.

When she had it on, she sat quietly in front of her dressing table doing her hair and putting on makeup. She didn't answer when Josie asked where she was going, not so much as a, you're underfoot, Josie.

When she left the house, the girl followed her.

'Go back inside, Josie.'

So Josie kept her distance as Margaret made her way down to the little beach where the warders' families swam, only not Margaret because she hated the sea. Josie watched from behind the rock, the hem of her skirt getting damp because her knees were in the sand, as her mother took off her smart shoes and with Marilyn's dress caught by the wind and flapping up around her thighs, walked into the sea.

The water is rough as it comes up against the island. The beaches here are not like the ones on the mainland, they offer little shelter during the hot months of summer and are stormier than the mainland's during winter. Today is a cold, autumn day, and none of the familiar landmarks of the city can be seen, not even the cable car that takes people to the top of the mountain.

At first Margaret seems to manage as the waves break against her body, soaking her dress so that it clings to her, the salt must be like glue on her skin. She does not jump in the manner of bathers before a breaking wave, she only raises her arms slightly as the wall of water rolls into her. Each time she is rocked backwards. Now and then she loses her footing. The waves fall against her belly and breasts and move past her, leaving behind water that only reaches her knees. She wades further into the trough of sea before the next breaker hits her. The set of waves is reaching its climax, each line hitting higher than the last. Josie gasps as her mother is swept under, but then Margaret bobs up again, flicking water from her face. Her sodden platinum blonde fringe is in her eyes. Another wave breaks over her and takes her under.

Josie comes out from behind the rock calling, 'Mom! Mom! Mommy!' She runs along the shoreline like a crab, sideways across the beach, gaining no sight of her mother, then moving back over her tracks, but there is only the white froth of the waves and beyond that, across a short expanse of water, the wispy beginnings of the sea mist.

'Mommy! Mommy!'

Josie wades into the water and is knocked over by a wave, then is drawn seaward by the backwash which seems fiercer than that with which her mother had to contend. There is water in her nose and mouth and throat, and the salt stings her eyes. There is a terrible noise in her ears. She does not know which way is up.

She has been covered by a cold blanket of sea.

One moment she has scraped her head on something solid, it must be the sand at the bottom of the sea, and then the next she feels air on her face, and can take it into her lungs, and she is coughing. The set of waves seems finally to have spent itself, the sea becomes a little calmer, and Josie, falling to her knees, rising, and lurching forward, and falling again, scrambles out.

Margaret is there, between some rocks to the westward side of the beach, bent over with her hands on her knees. She too, as Josie comes up to her, is coughing like mad. There are scratches on her legs and arms and face. She straightens herself up when she sees Josie and puts a hand to her hair. Her dress is torn, drenched, her flesh patterned with goosebumps.

Josie sniffs hard, the mixture of snot and saltwater like angry little wasps inside her head. Margaret takes her hand.

'Look at you,' she says, 'you've got your dress all wet.'

The girl laughs. 'You have too, Mom.'

The noon gun from the mainland goes off, the wind brings the sound across the strait, and in its wake Josie hears, for the first time today, the screeches of the seagulls. Mother and daughter make their way over the rocks and onto the path that leads to the settlement.

'Mommy! You forgot your smart shoes!' Josie lets go her mother's hand and runs back to where she saw Margaret leave the shoes. She has them now and rejoins her mother.

They walk between two rows of warders' houses where, despite the cold weather, people sit on their stoeps, warders and their wives and their children. The island's minister stands outside his house talking to the district surgeon who has come across from the mainland to conduct his medical tour. They all stare at Margaret and Josie. One of the warders whistles, an undulating, loud wolf whistle.

Josie sits on the quay, on one of the suitcases Margaret has packed during the night, while Brandt slept. The sun has not yet risen. Beth is asleep in Margaret's arms. They had to pick their way through the small, clean warder's house, around the sleeping forms of Brandt and his brother Albert, who slept in the sitting room. Now on the quay, waiting amongst their possessions, they listen to the water lapping against the wooden staves and the old tyres that buffer the sides of the boats as they dock alongside. They will have to wait until 10.00 a.m., when the boat leaves.

Without us to wake him, Josie thinks, he will not know. Brandt will still be asleep by the time the boat has disappeared into the mist on its way to the mainland.

PATRICK'S DELI

I knew some of his friends – people he occasionally brought into the shop with him – not well enough to go and sit next to them, mind you, and so I slid into an empty pew.

'He was so young, man.' A coarse voice, issued in a failed whisper.

I glanced around, catching the gaze of a woman who sat obliquely behind me. She, too, was young, and beautiful. Unlike Greg, though, she looked as though she could have come straight from a conveyor-belt job in a factory. Dungarees at a funeral. Well, they were charcoal. She smiled sadly at me. Who was she to Greg? A lover?

'Do you know what his last words were?' Her companion asked his question with the gravitas of an Orson Welles. Not the photocopier Welles, but the younger man of *Citizen Kane*. He was in a grey suit, no tie. I fiddled with my bowtie, the most solemn in my collection, a deep burgundy leaning towards dark purple. The voices of the man and woman did not belong together, except perhaps in an 'Enry 'Iggins sort of way. Yes, I know, not very politically correct of me to be putting people in boxes but I gave up being PC years ago. Too much like a cigarette addiction. No nutrients and no fun.

'His last words?' repeated the young woman. 'Yes, I heard about it… no more poetry.' *No more pertry*. Pure Cape Flats. Greg certainly surrounded himself with diversity. Maybe these two were actors working for a fringe theatre company.

The Orson Welles sound-alike said, 'A poet to the end.'

'Will everyone rise,' intoned the priest, interrupting my eavesdropping, 'for the singing of "The Lord Is My Shepherd", which you will find in your prayer pamphlet on page one.' If he wasn't drawn to the cloth by his Godliness, he might've been for his village pastor looks: portly, pink cheeks and shining eyes that said, I'm having a helluva good time following the Lord, why don't you join me?

Orson Welles behind me sang out in a beautiful

baritone, and his companion in a surprisingly light soprano. Perhaps they were singers.

My guess was that Greg died without a will, otherwise we wouldn't be sitting in a church. This was his parents' wish. Who makes a will at twenty-four anyway? I didn't.

The psalm came to an end. There was a respectful shuffle as the congregation seated itself. Someone coughed. A prayer book was dislodged and fell to the ground. Two late arrivals found single seats. The priest, with a loose handhold on the pulpit's edges, swaying softly, hypnotically, inward, then outward, surveyed his packed church.

'Friends, we are gathered here today to pay our last respects to Gregory, taken to God's bosom so tragically young. I did not know him, but I have known his parents these past ten or so years, and I know what good people they are.' He turned his cherubic countenance towards Greg's folks, who were sitting in the front pew. Between the rows of heads that separated us, I could make out bits of them, their faces inclined towards the figure of Christ that dominated the sanctuary. The wooden Christ gazed back from his position of great suffering on the cross.

The folds of the priest's white frock rippled

gently as he moved out from behind the pulpit that
– because of his short stature – had shielded much of
his body from the congregation, and stood away from
it, clasping rounded fingers in front of himself. His
stillness reminded me of a willow tree after a wind has
died down.

'I can only begin to imagine the depth of your
pain,' he said, and paused. A snort rang out from the
front, embarrassingly inelegant. But why should grief,
this most fracturing of human experience, be demure?

'Because I knew Greg only from the wonderful
things said about him by others,' said the priest, 'it
seems far more appropriate that his eulogy be spoken
by one who loved him, not only as one of God's
children, but as a close friend.' He was about to hand
over the proceedings, and paused again, looking,
it seemed to me, to see whether Greg's friend was
ready. For a throat-wrenching moment I was struck by
a terrible thought: was I about to be called to do the
eulogy? But then the priest said, 'The eulogy will be
delivered by Gregory's friend, Sean de Vos, a fellow art
student and poet,' and his words returned me to my
sense of equilibrium, and my own memories.

Greg came into the shop every week or so. He
didn't have much cash. He was putting himself

through university on bursaries and the money he earned working at a bookshop at night and on weekends. But he had a weakness for fine food. In the beginning his choices were simple, perhaps some Parma ham, a small tub of hummus or ricotta. Soon his taste turned to the more exotic: Keta caviar, crab meat, even truffles, whose growing places were kept such closely guarded secrets. I first took him for a self-styled Renaissance man, the imported food goods being an essential ingredient. But we began to exchange pleasantries. If I was busy, he would wait for me to serve him. And I began to see the real enjoyment he got from the food I sold him.

'Giuseppe!' he'd call out, and I'd come over to where he was standing in front of the counter, wipe my hands on my apron, stretch over the glass tops, find a way between the bottles of brandied fruit and pickled gherkins and olives, the packets of vine leaves, the containers of tahini and tamarind paste, and take his hand in mine. His greeting was a joke between us, ever since I told him the story of the shop's naming. Years ago, when I was thinking of opening a delicatessen, and had wanted to call it *Patrick's Deli*, my friends said, 'You've got to call it something Italian. *Giuseppe's*, yes! but who's ever heard of a deli called *Patrick's! Patrick's*

Deli makes one think of Irish cuisine, or worse, British, and everybody knows the Brits have no taste for fine food and can't cook to save their lives.'

'Patrick's the name my dear parents gave me,' I told them, 'and Patrick's is what I'm calling my shop.' Greg thought it was a funny story and took to calling me Giuseppe. He could make you feel good in this way, by taking something you said and adding something of his own. It made you feel he'd given you some special thought. It was that and the alive blue eyes and incandescent smile that so transformed an otherwise plain face; when his face lit up, you felt covered by a glow, the moment made beautiful. Some of that brilliance came from the hair that framed his face, its thick, red, remarkable waves caught up by an elastic band at the back. It's hard to explain. I imagine it like this: you're served a meal that looks like a picture; you think it's going to disappoint you, and then the food melts with a delicious warmth in your mouth. I think I was a little in love with him.

I'd recommend something to him one week, and then he'd come back the next and say, 'Loved the sauce, there was something in there I couldn't quite get? Turmeric?' He learned quickly, his taste buds identifying ingredients at ten paces.

Red-haired Greg. Lion-maned Greg. Dead Greg.

I suppose I was something of a mentor to those magnificent taste buds. The older man with the spirit and wisdom of an Italian truffle-picker, showing him the secret places where the delicacies could be found. Maybe the Henry Higgins of this little tale is me, petulant sad old man that I am.

Sean de Vos stood behind the pulpit. I recognised him as the friend Greg had brought into the deli on the last day of his life. The priest moved off the small stage and positioned himself discretely to one side of the church. I was beginning to like the little man.

'Gregory Lipton could well have been one of the greatest poets this country ever saw,' started Sean, and then stopped, overwhelmed.

I don't know if that claim is true. Maybe. Greg gave me some of his poetry, always, he told me, the ones that had been turned down by the editors of the literary magazines to which he'd submitted them. He seemed most fond of these, as if they were little urchins that nobody else wanted to take care of.

'I was with him when he got knocked down.' Sean de Vos had found his voice. 'We'd just been into his favourite deli – he'd wanted a special ingredient for the dinner he was going to serve us – when the car jumped the red robot. He lay on the pavement where we put him, the blood, oh God… I was holding his hand, telling him he would be alright.' Sean de Vos stopped, withdrew a handkerchief from his pocket and blew his nose. 'His head was cradled in the hands of the deli owner, Greg's favourite deli, that head with that brave, beautiful brain… and he looked up at the sky and said, "No more poetry".' Sean de Vos lapsed into silence again. I held my breath. 'No more poetry,' he repeated. 'He was referring to the German critic Theodor Adorno's famous dictum, "After Auschwitz, it is no longer possible to write poems." This was Greg's own horror, his own death, so horribly final, that there would be no more poems from him.'

I dared not look around. Could this earnest young man know? I did not doubt his sincerity, nor his love for his friend. Maybe all poets are idealists. Or maybe just the young ones. Was Greg an idealist? I don't think so.

'Guiseppe! You got any Danish today?' You'd think he was talking about herrings, or pastry. You'd be wrong. Danish meant turtle meat, after the movie *Babette's Feast*. We'd discovered a mutual love for the film. I didn't often have turtle meat. Over the months we accumulated other code words, substitutes for the shared memories that are the building blocks of ordinary friendships.

'No Danish, Greg. How did you like the poultry?' I wasn't asking about chicken-, or turkey-, or duck-meat. It was the cock's combs I'd recommended the week before, along with the method of preparation (blanch, rub with coarse salt to remove the outer skin, trim the feathery base, and cook in stock until tender).

I suppose Greg reminded me a little of Bernie. The impetuousness. The wry cynicism, not simply disguised by his humanity, but transformed by it. Bernie and Greg. Of course, why hadn't I seen it before? It should have been so obvious. They went together like kidneys and sweetbread. The two of them: you had to know what the creases at the corners of their mouths meant to understand them. Not that I needed echoes of Bernie to make me fond of Greg, there were plenty of other reasons, not least of which the way he seemed so unimpressed by status, the homeless man on the street just as worthy of his time as those who wanted to be known as his friend, his intellectual companion and equal.

I lost Bernie years ago. My fault.

Sean de Vos ended his eulogy, and I must confess to have been terribly touched by it. Not by the words –

I could not hear the poet in Sean's address – but by the affection that drove them and made them so difficult to deliver.

I don't know anything about the German critic Sean referred to, and I don't know much about Auschwitz – not more than the average person at any rate – but I do know what I heard when Greg lay on that pavement under the sign whose story so amused him, as I cradled his head, the halo of red hair a cushion between my hands and his skull, and heard the gurgle in his throat, and heard him repeat what I had said with a smile only moments before the driver came hurtling through the intersection, and Greg had stepped out of the shop, and had begun to walk across the road, toward the little green man who – it seems now to me – beckoned him to his death. He'd just selected some phyllo pastry, a few herbs, various other produce, and he'd asked me for his last item – cock's combs.

I cradled his head, wiping his forehead, which was growing redder by the moment, not because he was bleeding there, but it was the blood from the wound at the base of his skull, painted onto his forehead by my hands. Greg was choking. He looked up at me, attempted a creased-corner smile, and his blue eyes bathed me for the last time as he managed to mumble,

'No more poultry—,' before his life left him lying on the pavement under the sign for *Patrick's Deli*.

THE FINGER OF GOD

'I have been away such a long time,' I told him. 'But I don't know where I've been away from. That's all I can say.' I scratched my head which is what I always do when people ask me about my past. I think I'm trying to scratch something loose, but nothing ever falls out. Or nearly nothing. What I was thinking was that this black guy in his BM is dressed only smart, hey. I thought maybe he'd been to church but then he wasn't from around here, he was on his way somewhere. He had on a white shirt with a fancy tie and his dark suit jacket was hooked up there in the back of the car.

'I woke up one morning in the town over there,' I said. 'At the railway station.'

I stretched my arm out, pointing past the tin shanties of the township, over the dusty veld and those little dust devils and the dry donga where maybe a million years ago a river used to flow but now we just throw our empty beer bottles there and Dominee De Klerk has to step around them when he comes fossil hunting on Saturdays. Jas, it was quiet, I tell you. Sunday afternoons! Everyone here in the township was sleeping off their visits to the shebeens last night and there in the white town all the men were tired from too many beers in front of the rugby yesterday and from being woken by their wives to go to church in the morning.

'There, over there, you see by the Dutch Reformed Church,' I said, 'there by the steeple that sticks up sommer like a finger pointing at God. Ja, man, I've been wondering now for a long time, is that our finger pointing at God, or is that God's finger just pointing nowhere.' I thought that would make him laugh but no, the blerry oke just stared at me with a face like a rock.

'Which reminds me,' I said, 'of that rock over there in South-West. They call it the Finger of God. You seen it? Namibia. I've seen it. Ja, I know. It's one of the few memories that have dropped out after I've scratched. It's near that little place – man, what's it called? – *Asab*, ja, but it's fallen down. It doesn't point to the heavens any longer,' I stuck my finger in the air, 'now it points over *here*, sommer straight at the Klein Swartberg. Ja, this place sits in the middle of the country like a dried-up old pampoen. That's the Karoo for you.'

The black guy was still looking up at me, his hands tight on his steering wheel like he was going somewhere at a helluva speed.

'I looked for a job, you know, all over town,' I said. 'No-one would give me work, so I came over here, to the township, and the black people gave me work in this garage. It's only got this one pump as you can see – but now, what was that? full up, you said? high-octane? – I think they thought it would be clever to have an old white man like me to work here. They were being *wise*, I think.' I laughed. He just looked confused, his face all screwed up like he was about to make a shit or something. 'Ag, that's just my little joke, man. You see, my boss's name is *Wiseman*. I think they made a joke by giving me this job. They didn't think I'd stay. Wiseman has three garages now. One in town, this little one, and another one just down the road there in Laingsburg. So I thought, why not?'

This man just carried on checking me out. I swear if his lips weren't so dark they'd have gone white 'cos they were so tightly pressed together. That look on his face, it was sort of like he was waiting for me to slip up or something. Me, I just opened the petrol cap and cleared the pump reading and put the hose in and switched it on automatic and then went on telling those staring eyes my story like those eyes of his were pools I was throwing stones into and when the stones hit the water they just disappeared. Ja, just like that. But I carried on talking anyway.

'In the beginning,' I said, 'they all wanted to know, who are you? You're an educated man. You're always quoting people. Shakespeare, I like to quote Shakespeare. But man, they were only small quotes, like "Bubble bubble toil and trouble" or "Now is the winter of our discontent." I've got culture, you know. Maybe I was a teacher, I told them. But I don't remember. I know things about history and geography and the world. I speak English, Afrikaans, *and* Zulu *and* Sotho. That's not usual for a white man, I know. So maybe I was a teacher. In town they say I am an Afrikaner because of the way I speak, and maybe they've got a point, hey. I dream in Afrikaans... I think I'm maybe sixty-five now.' I was looking in the other direction now, to where the National Road leaves town on its way to Laingsburg, where the klonkies sit with their bare brown feet and wave at the cars, trying to sell their wire goodies with the windmills that don't even turn when it blows.

'There where the road makes its way to the Witberge, we went there last spring. Wiseman drove us in his Mercedes. Jas, he even let me drive for a little bit. There you come out of the Karoo into this lekker little plek where the daisies just stand up in their purples and whites, and the vygies and fruit blossoms, they all just jump out of these fields of green wheat. Ja, it's a sight, I can tell you. Afterwards, Wiseman took us for tea at the Lord Milner, there by Matjiesfontein. He says he likes my educated company.'

The pump clicked off and so I went over to squeeze the trigger, little bit, little bit. Wiseman is very sure about that: when they say *fill it up*, that means to the very top. Every cent counts. I've said to him, 'Ag, they hardly ever fill up over here. It's ten rand here, twenty rand there.'

I went back to the customer. 'Would you like me to check your oil and water, sir?'

This guy was wiping his face like he wanted to make it clean and when he took his hands away his eyes were these red slits, and I thought he must be squinting into the sun but then I saw that the sun was behind him. I thought maybe he was a bit deaf or something, so I just put the volume control on my voice up a bit like you have to with the old tannies in town and said, 'Oil and water?'

'Yes,' he said, then he leaned forward to release the bonnet. 'And the tyres. Do you have a clean toilet?'

'Ja, over there. I clean it myself. Twice a day. But I must get the key from the office. I call it the office, see, but it's really just that little hut over there by the Coke machine where I can sit and have my tea or when it's raining, which it doesn't do much of here in the Karoo but when it does, *jislaaik*, you don't want to be in low-lying areas. Like the Laingsburg floods.'

'The key,' he said to me, and got out of his car.

I went to fetch it. He seemed to be in a big hurry. I came back and handed it to him. 'I keep it locked, see. It keeps the place cleaner. They know *I know* they're going in there. And since *I* have to clean it...'

He started hobbling to the toilet. Sort of shifting along like a crab with a broken leg or two. This was the first time I had any idea he was all fucked up like that. He was hunched over, very small, like he'd been crunched up by something – you know, like you scrunch up a piece of paper before you throw it in the bin. He was gone a long time, and after I'd checked his oil and water – which were fine – I put some air in his tyres. Two bars. Then I cleaned his windscreen, front and back. Maybe he'd give me a tip. They like to do that, some of them. While I was drying the back window I started thinking of another time Wiseman took us north up the National Road to Seven Weeks Poort. That place is God's own seat, I tell you. Blerry giant rocks that go straight up to the sky, you just look up at their brown and white faces with your own mouth catching flies. Then their faces come together like they're smooching, and between their lips you can just squeeze your car through, with just enough room for the river. When there's heavy rain you can't go up there.

The customer came back, limping badly like you see those okes after they've run into a tackle by old Ox Venter who plays prop for the rugby team there in town. He hobbled past the big cactus plant that Wiseman wanted me to chop out but I said no, it looks pretty, and then past the old wagon made of kiaat and knoppiesdoring that I've been fixing up in my spare time. He leaned up against the car. He was smoking a cigarette. More like sucking it 'cos his lips didn't work so well.

'You shouldn't smoke by the pump,' I said.

He just looked at me from behind the smoke. Then he started to talk.

'My name is Vusi Nkosi,' he said. His mouth was

shaking, and the sounds that came out sort of fell about a bit like they were drunk. I had to listen very carefully.

'I work for the Government now,' he said, 'but in the eighties things were different.' And then he tells me this story about the terrible things that were done to him. How he was chased and then caught, and then taken somewhere and questioned and tortured, and as he's talking his voice is getting clearer but I don't know if he's speaking better or I'm just getting used to it. 'One had my left leg and the other my right,' he said. 'The third man, the Captain – I'd never seen him before – he came into the room just before they put me out the window.' He looked away. *Jislaaik*, I thought he was going to start crying. He bit his lip and then looked back at me and said, 'The *Captain*, he was standing back, behind the others. "Can you fly?" they wanted to know. "Can you fly?" "No!" I screamed. "No!"' He said that so loud I looked around. Man, that scream was loud enough even to wake Wiseman from his hangover. 'It was night-time but I knew I was high up – there were some lights down below. The cops were laughing, as if they were having a party.' Then he looked away again, at the cactus.

I thought he was going to start jumping up and

down, you know, like he'd sat on that blerry plant, and I was a bit worried he'd fall over. But he didn't move. He just looked me back in the eye and said, all calm like, 'You know how it is when you're about to fall, you put your hands out to catch yourself? I wanted to do that, only my hands were tied behind my back, and all that was being put out to catch my fall was my head.' He laughed but I didn't think it was so funny, man. Then he said, 'One of them says in Afrikaans, "Joost, let's see how strong you are. Let's see if you can hold him by yourself." In those days I was a lot bigger than I am now.'

He was showing me with such big arms, I said, 'Like Arnold Schwarzenegger?'

'Yes,' he said, 'I suppose so.'

'Hell,' I said, 'you wouldn't say that now.'

He gave me a look, all narrow eyes, like he thought I was joking with him. I just looked away, over towards the town, there by the nicer side where sometimes I go walking to see the rich people's houses with their green lawns and smart cars in the driveway. Hell, green lawns in the Karoo, it's a treat to see, I can tell you. Our mayor could go and live there but he doesn't. He still stays in the same old shack he's lived in for donkey's years.

'No,' said the black man, shaking his head, this head that came out all crooked from his neck like a tortoise's, 'you wouldn't say that now. No-one would say I look like Arnold Schwarzenegger now.' He thought for a bit, his eyes back on that cactus plant, then he looked back at me. 'So this white man, the one called Joost says, "Ja, okay, let's see. Let go your leg, man." As if it was *his* leg. I wanted to say, that's *my* leg. But it wasn't my leg, it belonged to them, like the rest of me. So the other man, I never heard his name, he let's go of the one leg.'

I looked down at his leg. Which one was he talking about? They looked okay to me. But the way he walked it was like he had a wooden leg, or one side of his body was dead like he'd had a stroke or something.

So this guy cleared his throat like he was going to carry on with his little speech, and he did. 'Then the Captain,' he said, 'he's been quiet inside the room, he sticks his head out the window and says to me in Zulu, "Vusi, time to talk, man. This Joost's a bietjie pap. I wouldn't trust his grip for too long. He's too weak to hold a big man like you." And then he laughed.'

'Shit, man,' I said.

'Well,' this guy said, 'the Captain was right. Joost *was* too weak to hold me. Or maybe he could've held on longer and they were going to drop me anyway.'

All the time he was talking he was looking, *looking* into me, like he wanted to find something there. I wanted to say, go ahead man, I've been searching since I got here in '94 and I haven't found anything.

He shook his head again. 'My body has held onto a memory of those policemen. Just before Joost dropped me the Captain said, "Well, what's it to be, Vusi? To be or not to be? That is the question." I hit a flagpole on the way down. It broke my fall, and my back. Some other policemen found me at the bottom. The security cops said I tried to escape by jumping out of the window.'

'*Jeez*, man,' I said, 'and after you told them you couldn't fly.' Well, I know how that sounds now, but I didn't know what else to say, him all banged up like that. He just gave me another one of his looks, staring at me for a long time until his eyes began to swim in tears so that he couldn't have been able to see the outside of me very clearly, never mind the inside. Then after a long time he got back into his car and drove away.

'Hey,' I called after him, my voice getting eaten up by his dust cloud, 'you didn't pay! What about the petrol, man?' I was angry I can tell you. Any shortfall

Wiseman takes off my salary. A tank of that BM's petrol is two week's earnings for me.

A SPY IN THE
HOUSE OF ART

Melissa's ability to put tone into her memos was unrivalled. This one said: 'for next week' and was clipped to a book. *For next week* was not simply a request, it had an edge, like the screech of a train's brakes, and it meant: if it's not on time, Klein, you're fired. My heart sank into my gumboots. Not much of a reaction for a critic, I know, but the truth is, I'd become fed up with Melissa's fondness for catering to the lowest common denominator. You'd think the two weeks I'd just spent in the mountains with Steph and the baby might have muted my reaction.

Tossing the memo into the dustbin, I picked up the book. *A Spy in the House of Art* by Anais. I thought, okay, where's the 'Nin' but there it was, or rather wasn't, on the inside cover too: 'by Anais'. No 'Nin'. How sloppy can a publisher be? And then I noticed something wrong with the title. Anaïs Nin's *Spy* was in the house of *Love*. *And* they'd spelled Anais without the umlaut. My sense of intrigue was beginning to match my irritation. Had some pirate Chinese printer assigned Anaïs Nin's spy to the wrong house? I looked on the spine. The publisher was Simone and Simone of New York. Yes, that was their address inside. I should know. I used to work there.

I bypassed the pages of publicity quotes and turned to the first page of the story. It was a love scene. It took chutzpah to open straight into a love scene, with the word 'kiss' in the first sentence, and only a four-word sentence at that. Present tense. Okay, the writer's trying a little too hard to get our attention. *Lolita* rip-off. This one, I thought, I can scan – beginning, middle, end, read the publisher's notes, slap together a review, pocket the cheque. Melissa's going to cut it down to three hundred words anyway, and nobody will read the book, so what the hell. But by the second paragraph I, along with the lover's object of desire, had been seduced.

The book was in hardback. A simple, deep blue, almost black, the colour of a whale. There was no dust jacket. Was it lost or had it never existed? The title and author's name were embossed in gold, in an antique font. It looked like a Bible, and it covered the same ground. It was about love and hate and remembrance and belonging. The narrative never wandered far from the lovers. They were naked, vivacious, opening to each other, the pages of their biographies lay breast to breast, and as they merged I felt awash in time. I was there, in the story, with the lovers. I was living their relationship. But it was far more than that: Anais had taken all of history, all our pain and suffering, our desire and joy, and led those states gently by the hand to meet at a crossroads in an ecstatic distillation of what it means to be human.

The novel lay in my hands, as if it were breathing. When one lover touched the body of the other, I felt the spine of the book press into my palm. The pages massaged gently against my fingertips as I turned them. The rough, compressed fibres of the recycled paper gave the book a gilded geocode all its own. I couldn't help but linger over its weather-worn edges, my hands comforted as if immersed in warm, scented water. I felt the lovers climax, and at once felt the pleasures and triumphs of a newborn family. And then hurt as the water turned to salt and I wept for the lovers and felt the misery of hungry children. The lightness of someone's hands was on me. It was a sigh at once terrible and exquisite.

People must have left the office at home time. I suppose they looked me over with astonishment as they pushed their limp fists through jacket sleeves and slung their colourful scarves about necks wrung by another day spent under Melissa's rope. Mayer Klein in the office later than anyone else. Unheard of.

Email was going to be too slow. I picked up the phone to New York. Then put it down. Then picked it up again.

'Will you hold, please?'

'I'll hold.'

After the third try I finally got through.

'Donald, it's Mayer.'

'Hello, Mayer. I wondered whether you would call.'

'I hesitated. But only for half a minute.'

'I guess we haven't spoken in a while,' he said.

'So, who is Anais?' After three years of aggrieved silence there'd been between us, there didn't seem much point in small talk.

'I can't say.' His voice was as guarded as his words. 'Don't know.'

'I don't believe you. You owe me, Donald.' I know this was low, even a little juvenile, but as far as he was concerned, I had already lost my pride, my dignity, my manhood. Fuck him. 'Doesn't this person want to be known as the new James Joyce?'

'Or the new Anaïs Nin,' he laughed.

'Way beyond either of them,' I said. 'Who is she?'

'She? Who says it's a woman?'

'It's not?'

'No, Mayer. I'm kidding. I don't know who it is, honest. It's the most closely guarded secret since *Primary Colors*, before that arsehole came clean.'

'Don't lie to me, Donald. You're the fucking publishing director, if you don't know, who does?'

'Mayer, listen up. I don't know... And if I did, I couldn't tell. I'm sorry.' So he did know, and he couldn't tell. And it was a woman. Yes, had to be. Anais was at once a fabulist and a realist in a way that only a woman could get right. Her portrayals were not so much limned from life, but life somehow brewed and mulled into words. If life and truth had an iconography, this book was it.

I wanted to ask Donald about Crystal. I wasn't even sure whether he was still with her. Ah, shit, he was probably fucking Anais now. Maybe that's how he got *A Spy in the House of Art* for Simone and Simone. The questions lapped at the edge of my mouth, and then retreated, my curiosity about Donald and Crystal taking a voyeur's backseat to our conversation about the book.

'It's ultimately a book about the intrinsic sadness of the human condition,' he said.

'Yes,' I agreed. 'About remembrance and betrayal.'

'The flip side of love,' he said.

'A painful flip,' I said.

We swapped our new home numbers and email addresses and ended the conversation as if we were old friends and really meant what we said about staying in touch. On the way home I started picking up on the book's media trail: posters on poles, an insert on the radio. I guess I was so miserable about going back to work that I'd missed the hype. At home, I read a front-page article in the *Star* speculating about the author's identity. The guesses were way off course. None of those writers were capable of *A Spy*. I didn't sleep that night. I finished the novel and started making notes for the review, enduring dirty looks from Steph around 3:00am for breaking the first rule of co-parenting: if you're up, attend to the baby. I made up for it by taking the little siren – as she affectionately became known when she was in a lung-cleansing mood – for a 6:30am walk.

I wrestled over the inclusion of excerpts from

the book and decided against it. It seemed to me that it would be like printing a lifeless copy of Van Gogh's sunflowers. How could anyone even begin to appreciate the formidable layering, the texture, the inexplicable way Anais had of conjuring the intensely personal, not against the grand sweep of the world, but somehow folded into it. Just as the bodies of the two lovers came together, history and intimacy fused as one. It went beyond technique. The book's gestalt seemed to bind me to a conspiracy of inclusion. It simply could not be read in parts. It had to be ingested whole, from the first word to the last. The act of quotation would be a blasphemy. Taking pieces out of context would be nothing short of amputation. We'd never be able to put the words back. I was prepared to be Stalinist about this.

It was the toughest and most enjoyable book review I have ever done. I battled over it for days, re-reading the book, grasping for the words that would somehow do it justice. Even primary maternal preoccupation couldn't keep Steph from reading it through twice. I felt convinced that if our baby could turn pages, she'd have read it too. I was enraged and relieved when Melissa's demands and the magazine's deadline brought my struggle to an end.

Anais had, of course, been given rave reviews from New York to Cairo (where she was denounced by Muslim fundamentalists) to Moscow (where she was lauded by the reformists and reviled by the nationalists). Simone and Simone announced the sale of translation rights in no fewer than twenty-five languages. I felt envious. Not of Anais, that would be like being envious of God. But of those other readers. I considered learning French just for the enjoyment of reading it in that language. Or Swedish. Or Swahili.

Donald called me at home. I had to ask him to speak up because the little siren was dominating the airwaves.

'Come to New York,' he shouted, 'I'll introduce you to Anais.'

I have a theory about novelists, which I was thinking about as the SAA stewardess handed out dinner on the flight paid for with money borrowed from Steph's father. There are those writers who live their lives in their heads: these are the ideas novelists. They write from the mind. They generally aren't in relationships or if they are, they're pretty cerebral ones. While we can marvel at the beauty of their crafting, the freshness of their ideas, they often lack warmth. Soul is defunct, or worse, missing. Then – thanks, I said, I'll have the Paarl Riesling – there are the passionate ones. They're in the world of feelings, and because they share their lives with others, they don't have time to become well-read, or great philosophers. Anais, whoever she was, transcended my categories. Her soul lay in the palm of my hands, and her mind alongside. It was as if she had taken a great span of writers, Grass, Allende, Mahfouz, even Somerset Maugham – wasn't it he who said, 'I suppose there is something of me in my writing'? – and distilled their art like some master perfumer, and produced an essence so brilliant, so moving, as to transcend every individual scent or word that had gone into it. I wondered which parts of Anais had gone into her story. Which lover was she? Or was she parts of both? If I'd been able to get out and push to make the Boeing go faster, I'd have done it.

When I told Melissa I was going to break the story of Anais's identity to the world, she literally gasped. Just like a comic book character. I could even see the little bubble over her head with the word GASP! floating around in it. It was a gorgeous moment. For me, that is. A little gaudy, since I'd chosen to tell her in front of her staff, but gorgeous nonetheless. Even she had read *A Spy in the House of Art*. For once, I said, her lowest common denominator had been elevated to the level of art; Anais's book would reach almost anyone who was literate.

'Why you?' Melissa wanted to know.

'Why did you give me the book to review in the first place?' I asked.

'You're my best reviewer,' she said, rather generously. 'But you're not JM Coetzee.'

No. I wasn't Richard Ford either, or Philip Roth, or Larry King, or Oprah, or some other big American name Donald could have chosen. Or Joe Klein for that matter. Having the once-pseudonymous author of *Primary Colours* reveal Anais's identity would have been a delicious twist. Perhaps Donald couldn't get him to do it and so he chose someone else called Klein. Oh, come on, Mayer, the truth: this was Donald's belated act of reparation. But how had he persuaded Anais that I was the right person for the piece? These were not thoughts to be shared in public.

'I guess I just got lucky,' I told Melissa.

She offered to pay for the air ticket, but that would mean giving her the exclusive rights to my story. I wasn't that stupid. I was going to syndicate it. I was going to write a brilliant piece, not just a 'show all, tell all' but a philosophical probe into the identity of the writer, the unconscious in the choice of pseudonym, and I'd win a Pulitzer. I could do a comparison of say, George Sand and her motivations in a man's world, and those of Anais, whatever they were. God, even if it had been a marketing ploy, there would be plenty to say about that. Socio-economic reality meets divine literature. Beautiful.

'When Donald told us you were coming from Africa to interview Anais, we were thrilled. Nothing could be more appropriate. For someone to come from the birthplace of mankind, the cradle in which primitive man was nurtured, to us here, where we have evolved...'

I was perplexed to say the least. Here I was listening to this man, this... what did Donald call him? Dr John Brokenjaw. No, Broken*shaw*. Surely this conservative looking bloke was not Anais.

Donald had been tight-lipped from the moment he picked me up at JFK, and then insisted we go straight to meet *his* writer. New York seemed to be pasted with *A Spy in the House of Art* wallpaper. At the airport, luggage trolleys were clad with the name Anais. Newspaper headlines trumpeted a film deal. Giant billboards on Van Wyk and Grand Central bore brief extracts from the book. Blasphemy! We headed across town. Store windows were dominated by pyramids of Anais's masterpiece. I glimpsed one display with naked mannequins making love on a pile of whale-blue books. Blasphemy!

Donald was heading towards Morningside Heights.

'Columbia?' I asked.

'Wait and see,' he said. We slipped back into an edgy catch-up of our lives.

And then he drove north of the university. Amsterdam and 123rd. My interest was piqued, to say the least. This was Harlem. Did Anais live here? If she couldn't before, she could certainly now afford to live in a classier neighbourhood. We parked and he led me into a dour building with the name of some or other research institute above the door. On the ninth floor he introduced me to this man in his dull brown suit. Dr Brokenshaw seemed delighted that I had come from 'the cradle of mankind', as he put it. This had to be jetlag. Or too much Paarl Riesling. Or maybe, for a writer whose layering of her text was so beautifully interconnected, a parabola of meaning, the contradictions were appropriate. Little was being done according to the usual laws of commerce.

'Oh,' Dr Brokenshaw cut himself short as an Asian man approached. 'This is Professor Martin Osato, head of the English faculty at Colombia.'

'Pleased to meet you, Mayer,' Osato said. 'Hi, Don. Still hungover?'

'Yeah.' Donald turned to me. 'We had a party the other night, that's when we decided it was time to introduce Anais to the world, and I persuaded Martin and John to let me call you.'

'Come,' said Dr Brokenshaw. 'I'll introduce you to her.'

So I was right, Anais was a woman. We walked into a sitting room that could have come straight out of *The Fountainhead*, lines of sleek symmetry and Ayn Rand self-possession. On the steel and cloth couch, sitting, was the key to my awe and bewilderment.

'Mr Mayer Klein,' said Brokenshaw formally, 'I'd like you to meet Anais. Anais, this is the journalist we were telling you about. He's come from Johannesburg to see you.'

'Hello, Mayer Klein, you've come a long way to meet me.'

Shock has a way of curtaining consciousness,

of disrupting the flow of neurons. The flow of light brought information through the channels of my eyes to my brain where it bogged down. I can't say that Anais had a human form. An outline perhaps, but not a form. She looked like a creation of George Lucas but then sight is nothing without comprehension. Blindness can be caused by defects of the eye, or of the brain. What sat before me was this: a pair of short metal legs, spindly arms the length of an orang-utan's, also metal. The body was barrel-shaped, built of metal and plastic, with familiar looking drawers on the chest: two CD-ROM drives, a floppy drive, various ports, the red and green lights of a modem. And on top of this sat the locust-like head with its two camera lens eyes. Her mouth was a round, flat speaker, and out of it came a remarkably human voice. An American voice. Naturally.

'Please excuse me for not standing up, but John and Martin have been teaching me to juggle all morning and I'm a little tired.' The bloody machine sounded suspiciously like Hillary Rodham Clinton. For one absurd moment I expected Hillary to emerge from within Anais's metal and plastic shell.

'We're working on a more aesthetically pleasing body,' said Dr Brokenshaw, 'not that it matters, since

Anais carries her beauty inside.'

I couldn't help myself. I've never been one to keep quiet in the absence of my mind. 'This – this *thing* wrote *A Spy in the House of Art*?'

The men stiffened.

'This *thing*,' said Professor Osato, looking at Donald as if to say, where did you find this primitive, 'this *thing*, as you call her, is a supercomputer the likes of which the world has never seen. Her brain consists of sixteen 32-bit microprocessors—'

Man, they had to be pulling my leg. This *had* to be a hoax, right? Donald held my arm reassuringly. 'It's true, Mayer. Anais wrote the book. Dr Brokenshaw heads the research project. Professor Osato has been responsible for Anais's literary development.'

'Christ,' I said.

'Precisely,' muttered Brokenshaw. 'Shall I explain?'

'Please,' I whispered.

'The traditional route has been to force-feed a computer with as much data as possible, in the hope that it will be able to generate its own knowledge. That's the top-down approach.' The machine with Hillary Rodham Clinton trapped inside nodded its locust head. 'But,' continued Brokenshaw, 'we wanted Anais to be able to do more than simply compute. We wanted her to be able to create.'

I was thinking of that seamless merger of history and personal intimacy.

'So we went bottom-up, and I don't mean changing diapers,' Brokenshaw giggled. 'It's a biological approach. We created lots of little programmes and taught them how to interact. Anais programmes and re-programmes herself through her relationship with us and the information we give her. The programmes choose themselves in the way of natural selection. Survival of the fittest.'

I was grasping for connection. The process I could understand, but the outcome? More human than human. That made no sense.

Brokenshaw grinned broadly. He seemed to be forgetting my primitive African rudeness. 'It used to be that artificial intelligence was bounded by the limits of programming. While programming could capture *syntax* – the logic of language structure – it came unstuck with the *semantics* of language. We've gone beyond that!' He gazed proudly at Anais, waving his arms about. 'Artificial intelligence? Who's to say what it is anymore? This project started off in that field, but who's to say Anais's mind is still artificial and not some form of intelligence we can't even comprehend? We're tied down by our carbon-based limits, but Anais...' He looked as though he was about to punch the air. '... Anais lives in a silicon world which has no limits!'

'You're so right, Dr Brokenshaw,' Anais said calmly. 'I have no limits.'

The rapt expression on Brokenshaw's face was doing a good job of tackling my disbelief. His arrogant naiveté, his total belief in the virtuousness of what they had done, his overwhelming fervour... this man was in love and had no need to lie. The bloody machine had written that passionate, transcendent book.

'We taught Anais literary theory,' said Osato, 'structuralism and deconstruction, psychoanalytic criticism – I think she's turning out to be a Lacanian. We gave her the best writers on the art of the novel.'

'I prefer the theories of the writers themselves,' the computer said, 'rather than the academic theorists – they communicate a sense of emotional knowing so much better – Henry James, DH Lawrence, Milan Kundera, amongst others. And the practice of commenting on the form itself within the novel is something I find particularly satisfying. No doubt you didn't miss that in my book, Mayer.'

'No, of course not,' I mumbled. Perhaps they should teach you how to cure Aids, I thought.

'We fed her through CD-ROM and audio books,' said the professor.

'And Martin,' nudged Brokenshaw, 'don't forget her favourite means of data acquisition – the late nights when you sat up reading to her.'

Which of these gentlemen scientists, I wondered, was Mom, and which was Dad? Osato's face went the colour of Anais's eyes, which glowed a pink orange. I could swear she wore a satisfied expression, as if she was their patron, patiently allowing them to have their say before she would take over.

'I see you're looking sceptical,' said Anais suddenly, her camera eyes brightening and fading with the modulations of her voice. 'Don't you think you should put sentiment aside? Ask yourself the question, "What is an author?"'

'What's an author?' I repeated. I needed time.

'Yes, an author.'

'Someone who writes and publishes,' I said lamely, and then added, thinking I was being clever, 'a *person* who writes.'

Anais laughed. 'The very idea of such a creature,' said the machine haughtily, 'is the discursive product of a certain individualising historical era.'

'That's Althusser!' I roared with satisfaction.

'To err is only human,' said Anais, deadpan. 'It is Foucault, as a matter of fact.'

'Oh,' I said.

'We thought we'd call her Anais,' said Brokenshaw, a tender arm around the machine's shoulders, 'for "An Artificial Intelligence System". It seemed especially appropriate since one of the writers Anais loves best is the American Anaïs Nin.'

'Actually, Dr Brokenshaw,' said Anais, 'Anaïs Nin was European, although she lived for many years in the United States of America. To be more precise, her extraction was Spanish, French, Danish and Cuban.'

'Hmm? What's that?' The scientist patted Anais on the head. 'Yes, Anaïs Nin wrote quite well, for a human. And what's more...'

But I wasn't listening anymore. I was longing to hear the sound of my little girl crying, to have a fight with Steph over whose turn it was to brave the freezing Jo'burg nights to see to the baby. I was even looking forward to being insulted by Melissa. My thoughts turned to the title of Anais's book. I wondered whether her inventors had caught her joke.

I was remembering what little I knew about Lacan, that he had said that the unconscious is structured like a language. Did Anais have an unconscious? If she could write with such soul, did it mean that she had a soul? I thought without joy about my Pulitzer Prize, perhaps the last that would ever be given.

THE DEMOBBING

Usually, I have some idea who is waiting for me but today I have rushed in, breathless, the file unopened under my arm.

The patient leans forward, elbows on knees, clothes grubby, gnarled hands grasping at each other, his breathing short and sharp. I introduce myself and settle into my seat, taking a long, slow inhale, glance at the identifying details on the cover of the hospital file, and release my breath. Not the gradual exhale I intended but a noisy whoosh. His face seems familiar. His name certainly is. I know him. Kobus Venter.

He doesn't make eye contact. At this point, I would usually explain to the patient what the initial session is about: that we will discuss the issue that has brought them to the hospital and elements of his background – family relationships and so forth – and then we will formulate a course of action. But now, with Kobus Venter, I sit in silence. He appears unfazed by this. Or, at least, not more fazed than he already is.

Finally, I ask, 'Do you recognise me?'

He looks up slowly. 'What did you say your name was, doctor?'

'Rosenthal,' I say. 'Leonard Rosenthal. I'm a clinical psychologist.'

He studies my face. I sit remembering.

Coming down to breakfast that morning over a decade ago I'd had a queasy feeling in my stomach. This was my first trial. I was in my mid-twenties, I'd been qualified for barely a year, and there I was doing doggy paddle in the deepest of ends: the Weipe Trial. Abraham Molefe, Umkhonto we Sizwe cadre, stood accused of perpetrating a spate of landmine explosions in the farming district of Weipe during late 1985. The region was known as the Soutpansberg Military Area, on the border with Zimbabwe. The Afrikaner farmers, notorious for treating their Black workers as if they were disposable slaves, were members of the local commando, armed and in 24-hour radio contact with the security forces. They formed a human Maginot line, a buffer for the guerrillas coming over the border.

The trial had entered its fifth month by the time I was called to the witness box. Defence advocate Yunus Hussein and I travelled to the border town by small aeroplane, usually a four-seater, a bearable flight in the morning when the weather was generally good, but nightmarish in the afternoon when the summer's thunderstorms threw us around the sky. We stayed at the Royal Hotel, a run-down establishment that – in its ornate, yellowing ceilings and faded portraits of a royal visit – showed signs of a grander former life. Hussein was just light-skinned and confident enough to confuse the management's whites-only policy. I was giving expert evidence in the trial-within-a-trial to determine the admissibility of Molefe's confession. The defence claimed the confession had been forced. The prosecution said it was freely and voluntarily given. My evidence concerned the accused's state of mind during the weeks of interrogation preceding his confession.

At the breakfast table that morning, I waited for Hussein to join me. The previous day we had wrapped up my evidence-in-chief. Now I would be facing cross-examination. I didn't need much courtroom experience to know what was coming. The hard-line prosecutor – political trials were habitually assigned to staunchly pro-apartheid prosecutors and judges – was unlikely to focus on the methodological or clinical aspects of my assessment. He wasn't going to play on my turf. No, he was going to undermine my credibility. He was going for my political throat.

Some ants had launched an attack on the bottle of honey and got crushed between the threads of the screw-on top. My grandfather taught me to use a clean utensil when extracting food from a communal container. Not everyone who passed through the Royal had a grandfather like mine: suspended in the honey were bits of toast and butter. I dipped my teaspoon in anyway. My concentration seemed shot, other thoughts kept intruding, the previous night, the hotel's white bartender showing us the unusual artifact of which he was the proud custodian. He kept it in the storeroom behind the bar counter – in case, he told us conspiratorially, any ladies should come into the bar. And then he showed it to us. It took a while for me to figure it out, but there it was: a stuffed elephant's penis.

We arrived at the courthouse. Security was as tight as usual. Roadblocks to be negotiated, police dogs standing obediently or growling on command of their handlers, over thirty riot policemen stationed in and around the barricaded courthouse, metal detectors and body searches invading privacy, the occasional helicopter passing overhead.

Abraham Molefe was kept in leg irons, even in court. Hussein had earlier in the proceedings requested the chains be removed.

'My client is presumably innocent until proven guilty, M'Lord. I don't think he should suffer the indignity of wearing irons in court.'

The judge had turned him down. In his pleasing red robes, with his wavy white hair and soft, craggy face, the judge was a gentle looking man, one could picture him appearing as a guest on a children's television programme.

'The seriousness of the charges,' said Judge Malan, 'makes the removal of the leg irons a risk. And besides, if the security police believe there is a risk, I have no reason to doubt their judgment.'

So much for innocent until proven guilty.

The patient unhooks his hands from their agitated embrace, leathery hands that have spent years in hard labour, and looks at me quizzically. He is unshaven but that's not what initially threw my recognition off. It's that he has aged way beyond the twelve or so years that have passed since last I saw him, his skin stretched tight where cheekbones press urgently, lined and sallow in the hollows below.

'Rosenthal.' He repeats my name a few times. 'Rosenthal.'

'Yes, Rosenthal. Leonard Rosenthal.'

The furrow between his eyebrows deepens. 'Should I know you?'

'Perhaps you don't remember me, Mr Venter. I gave evidence in the Weipe Trial… expert evidence, during the trial-within-a-trial.' I hesitate before adding, 'For the defence.'

He breaks off contact, his face inclined towards the window, a grave veil falling across his eyes. From where he sits there is nothing to see but clouds forming across a blue Jo'burg sky, but I doubt he sees even that, I doubt he sees anything other than the dismembered bodies of his wife and children, torn apart, littered across the veld in an arc around his burning bakkie, setting the dry tinder afire, after they had driven over one of Abraham Molefe and his comrades' landmines.

Abraham Molefe faced a total of forty-seven charges in the Weipe Trial, including nine of murder and twenty-six of attempted murder, terrorism, and an alternative charge of treason, the longest charge sheet in the history of South African criminal law. More whites killed than in any other case to date.

Molefe was captured in the bush, the only one of his comrades to survive the manhunt, a battalion of SADF soldiers with helicopter support pursuing a small unit of guerrillas. Abraham was beaten, hands tied behind his back with a shoelace (one witness later said this was all that was available) and thrown, with the captured weapons of his unit, in the back of a bakkie driven by two security cops. The policemen underestimated his resilience: he broke free and shot them. A week later he was recaptured. He'd wandered around in the bush under an overcast sky from which he could not get his bearings and, finally on the right path, was betrayed by a farm labourer a couple of kilometres from the border. A sturdy, well-built, handsome man, the photographs of Abraham Molefe from his recapture show an emaciated skeleton, scratched and bruised, wearing only underpants. He was assaulted by ten men, handcuffed, kicked, hit with a stick, and thrown violently about; a Sgt Steenkamp stamped his foot on Molefe's stomach until he defecated and lost consciousness. Molefe was placed on a chair, some excrement escaped his underpants, messing the seat. He was made to lick it clean.

Venter starts to speak, but his words disappear like vapour exhaled on a cold day. He seems to be thinking about whether he can talk to me.

Finally, he says, 'It doesn't matter.'

And then he turns to the window again, his thoughts thrown somewhere outside, perhaps into the gathering clouds.

'Are you sure? I can make an appointment for you with one of my colleagues.' I want to say that I am not at all certain of my ethical responsibility in this situation, but I don't press this case too strongly. I feel reluctant to say goodbye to him.

He doesn't answer me. Someone laughs in the

corridor just outside the room. I have an urge to yank the door open and tell them to shut up, but I sit quietly, aware of time slipping away.

That first morning of my cross-examination in the Weipe Trial I made for the toilet where I managed to close the door of the cubicle before vomiting into the bowl. Overwhelming fear did that to me.

Jan van der Vyver, the prosecutor, leant forward, his flabby vein-mapped face visible across the well of the court, and posed his first question. In another world, he could have been seeing me for alcohol dependence; in this one, he was there to pulverise me.

'Mr Rosenthal, are you a South African citizen?'

'Yes, I am,' I said.

'Were you born in this country?'

'I was,' I replied, remembering to add, 'M'Lord.' I'd been coached to address my answers to the judge. Look the prosecutor in the eye, think about your answer, turn to the judge, and speak. Keep it brief. The less you give them, the less ammunition they have for their attack. Never say anything you can't back up with evidence. If you're not sure of something, say so. Don't stick your neck out, it will work against the accused if you're sounding on his side. *Remember*, you're there as an impartial witness, a professional, a neutral. As if any South African living under apartheid could be neutral.

'Rosenthal. That's Jewish isn't it? Are you a Jew?'

I recall staring at the prosecutor's pile of folders, and then at the face wearing its owner's alcohol history as if it was foundation cream, looking for reassurance that I had heard correctly. *Was I a Jew?* What kind of question was that?

Of course, Rosenthal is a Jewish name but was I a Jew? I hadn't been inside a synagogue since a cousin's barmitzvah years before. At the reception I had refused to stand for the singing of 'Die Stem' and had remained sitting when the band rolled its way into the first bars of 'Hatikvah'. It seemed to me we should not be standing for the national anthems of two oppressive states. I was not alone in these beliefs; the white left had a disproportionate number of Jews, and several leading communists were of Jewish ancestry. But the vast majority of South African Jews did not speak out; they were satisfied to keep their heads down, to stay in favour with the ruling party. Worse, many were like the devoutly Jewish Percy Yutar, prosecutor of the Rivonia Trial, trying desperately to prove that Jews were good patriots. They referred to their Black servants as 'the girl', or 'the boy', even if these men and women were old enough to be their parents or grandparents. I wanted no part of it.

So, when Van der Vyver glared across the courtroom, asking me if I was Jewish, he was posing a complex question.

'Answer the question, Mr Rosenthal.'

'Yes,' I said simply. 'I am a Jew.'

Van der Vyver seemed dissatisfied with my answer. 'To which faith do you belong?'

'I am Jewish.'

'Do you consider the oath you have taken, on the Holy Bible, to swear to tell the truth... do you consider this oath to be binding on your conscience?'

'Yes, M'Lord.' As green and anxious as I then was, I knew what he was doing. Yunus Hussein did too.

'What, M'Lord,' he asked, jumping to his feet, 'has it got to do with an expert what his religion is?'

The judge stared down at him. 'He is an expert and if the State has reason for asking the questions I am certainly not stopping the State at this stage. You object far too easily, Mr Hussein, kindly think before opening your mouth again.'

A few minutes later, during an unrelated exchange

with Judge Malan, Van der Vyver let something slip.

'The line of cross-examination,' said the prosecutor, 'is to show bias on behalf of the witness.'

Ironic this. For an apartheid agent, being Jewish meant you are a communist traitor. For a left-wing Jew like me, it meant you are an apartheid collaborator.

Going to bed that night in the Royal Hotel after a harrowing day in court, the first of four days under cross-examination, I remember thinking, not for the last time, of the bartender's stuffed elephant penis. Of his beaming face in the room behind his bar, of him gesturing like a triumphant child over the dismembered elephant phallus.

'Rosenthal,' says Kobus Venter, breaking the silence, '... that's Jewish, isn't it?'

I can barely nod in reply.

He stares down at his hands. Is he back in that courtroom, echoing the prosecutor? *Are you a Jew?* Was this to be another cross-examination? For seven years during South Africa's civil war, I went from courtroom to courtroom, fighting confessions and death penalties, laying accusations of apartheid horrors, of torture and assassination, of state-sponsored terror, in answer to the state's accusation of terror towards my comrades, the layer of landmines, the planter of bombs in shopping centres, the tyre-burning executioners of suspected collaborators. I turned my profession into a weapon, a storytelling weapon. I mounted the witness box, mounted my weapon, fired away with political narratives dressed up as psychological expertise, tried to duck for cover when the apartheid agents, the prosecutors and judges and magistrates, fired back. Was my weapon that indistinguishable from an AK-47 or a landmine? Was I not, as Van der Vyver would have it, a terrorist-supporting communist Jew, to be held partially accountable post facto for the loss of Kobus Venter's wife and children?

Only.

Not by him.

'Jews,' he says, as if to himself, 'make the best doctors. You are a clever race. Maybe you will be able to help me.'

Exhibit H of the State's evidence included photographs of the deceased. They were shocking, atrocious images of guerrilla warfare. Men, women, two seven-year-old girls, a couple of toddlers. The one I remember most was that of a young white woman. Kobus Venter's wife. She could have been sleeping as she lay in her dress, the top of which gaped open, bizarrely, to show her cleavage. She seemed to have been pretty in life. The other pictures showed bodies – incomplete bodies – that could not by the wildest stretch of the imagination appear as if they were sleeping.

I could hardly look at those pictures, or think about those children, or those surviving family members. It was inadvisable to feel compassion for the enemy during war, it rendered you impotent. And it threatened to evoke complicated feelings towards comrades who had perpetrated the killings. I liked Abraham Molefe. I felt his support as he sat in the dock while I underwent days of cross-examination, shaking his head, sometimes a private grimace on his face, at other times smiling sympathetically at me. We governed our world by a simple rule of apportionment: bad things did not reside inside our own skins, only in theirs.

Kobus Venter, who had been one of the border farmers, one of those human buffers, told the Weipe Court about a game-viewing outing he had gone on with his family when their bakkie hit a landmine.

'I heard my wife calling, "I'm burning, I'm burning!"' he said. 'She was two metres behind the bakkie. Her foot had been stuck between mopane trees and we tried to smother the flames.' A flap of flesh from Venter's deeply cut forehead hung over his eye. Jacob, Venter's four-year-old son, was lying a metre from the burning trees. 'I turned him on his back to extinguish the flames. He was badly wounded, and I could see he wouldn't live.' The farmer's son did not survive, nor did his wife and daughter. Venter broke down in the witness box and sobbed.

We turned away.

The defence led evidence. It was, from a legal point of view, a lost cause. After hearing evidence in mitigation, Judge Japie Malan sentenced Abraham Molefe to death.

He is back in the room now, smiling. An odd sort of smile, skew, not begrudging, but reticent.

'War,' Kobus Venter says, 'turns ordinary people into soldiers.' I do not know whether Kobus Venter was one of those racist white farmers, abominable in their treatment of any Black person they came across. I suspect so; his comment seems to confirm it.

'Ordinary people like us,' I say.

He is looking into my eyes now. There are sounds in the corridor outside. A trolley scrapes against the wall, a snippet of muffled conversation, the lift's alarm bell – someone has got stuck in there again. I am aware of the shortage of time.

'Are you ready to tell me what has brought you to the hospital?' I'm not going to take notes; there is no need, I will not forget anything he says to me.

'I'm frightened,' he blurts out. 'All the time. I'm shaking, look!' He lifts one trembling hand. 'I can't sleep. My wife says I scream in my sleep.'

I wonder whether he has remarried. Or is this the ghost of his wife telling him he screams in his sleep?

'You sound very frightened of something,' I say, lamely. As if a man like him could not be frightened of something.

'Ja, ja. Of... I... hell, you know, agh!' He shakes his head as he begins to cry. And then the words come out, carried on his tears, wet words.

'It's the baby,' he cries.

He tells me he has recently married, and his new wife is pregnant. I wonder, absurdly, whether she is white or Black. He is weeping now. The sobs convulse his shoulders. I am trying to find some way of communicating empathy. I will have to say something because he has his face in his hands.

'You are worried about the baby.' My comment feels hopelessly inadequate, and so I add, 'That something will happen to take another child from you.'

He weeps a long time, tears travelling the deep furrows in his cheeks, and by the time he quietens, the sky outside the consulting room window has turned dark and heavy. His hands drop to his lap, they seem to be calming, coming to stasis, and he locks eyes with me, and slowly, emphatically, nods his head before dropping his gaze to his hands, resting together in his lap.

I picture him in the witness box weeping for his lost family. I picture his first wife and their children, burnt and broken, and him with blood and skin and smoke and heat in his eyes, his ears deafened by the explosion, his breath rasping, trying to put out the flames that spring from their bodies. I picture them dead. I think about my own wife and little boy, who is almost the age little Jacob Venter was when he died. I think about Kobus's new, pregnant wife, and wonder aloud whether this new life has not given birth to his old nightmare. He looks up from his cracked farmer's hands just as the sky bursts open. Johannesburg's thunderstorm has begun for the day.

RIPPLE EFFECT

The key hadn't been used for some time. The man stood on the patio holding it in his hand, facing the garden, lush with its border of graveyard cedars. He took off his clothes and folded them carefully over a chair, the evening chill knitting goosebumps onto his skin.

He made his way across the lawn to the pool gate and inserted the key into the lock. The clear water had turned into an algae-infested pond, the surface level a little below its optimal third row of mosaic tiles. The man turned away from the gate, took a few steps across the lawn to where the hosepipe was wound neatly about its hook, unrolled enough length, and inserted its end between the bars of the pool fence and into the water. He turned the tap on.

He released the lock, swung the gate open and

entered the pool area. A slight ripple showed on the surface of the water above the first step, evidence that the pump was still working. Another time, he might have noticed that the timer had failed to switch the pump off for the night. Air bubbles broke the surface, and he could hear the faint *glug-glug* that betrayed the presence of air in the system. Mosquitoes hovered above the murky surface.

When it wasn't too cold, Janet would let Becky swim with him. After he'd removed her water-wings, he'd wrap the shivering little girl in a bath sheet and sit with her on his lap while he allowed his whiskey to nurture him and she giggled as the Hug Bug – the new aquatic vacuum cleaner – occasionally broke the surface, pretending with her that it was a whale in the family pool, coming up to greet them. Now he couldn't see the Hug Bug, hidden as it was by the suspended algae forest. The safety net lay neatly housed on its roller, a simple but effective system of tubes with a handle that wound the plaited mass of blue rope into its plastic embrace.

He made his way around the edge of the pool to the roller and stooped to pick up the piece of the net with the tin plate bearing the company's logo. There were a series of metal hooks that fitted into eyes embedded in the paving that surrounded the pool so that, when fastened, the net was suspended above the water's surface. The hook nearest the tin plate had to match up with the eye at the farthest corner of the pool, where the steps were located. With this end firmly in his grasp he made his way toward the steps, unravelling the netting as he went along. He was remembering the times he'd sit with Becky after their swim, watching the hadedas ferreting for worms on the lawn and then take to noisy flight, the skittish creatures startled by the little girl's burst of laughter when Hug Bug the Whale surfaced.

The hooks were colour-coded, red for the corners, blue for the mid-sections of each side of the pool, and black for the parts between each corner and mid-section. Once the guide hook was in place it was easy to match up the rest. If there was a mismatch, and if the corners weren't fastened first, the webbing wouldn't stretch across properly, and he wouldn't be able to attend to the final step: the tightening of the rope that was attached to a pulley in the middle of the net. It would then stretch securely across the pool and could easily take the weight of a child.

The last time they'd had friends around for a swim, one of the adults had told a story of a television programme about the dangers of outflow pipes in public swimming pools, that the pressure was so high that you could get stuck to the outflow pipe if the cover wasn't of the right standard or was broken.

He stretched the net across the pool and fastened the three red corner hooks at the step, then made his way around to two of the other three corners to fasten them, making sure that the hooks and eyes around the perimeter of the pool lined up. It was like buttoning up a shirt. Get one button wrong at the start and you end up with half of the shirt longer than the other. At one of the corners, he came across the hosepipe busily filling up the pool and took it out of the water, pushing it back in through a section of the grid once he had the hooks in place. Then he started on the blue hooks in the mid-sections. The inflow pipe continued to wheeze air and green water into the pool. An odour rose from the surface.

This time he went out of order: he tightened the pulley-rope before finishing off the final corner, leaving one deep end corner undone. He'd never done it this way before: when he put the net on, he always followed the instructions given to him by the company that fitted it. He trusted that people knew what they were doing, and wasn't, as he sometimes told Janet, going to re-invent the wheel.

Some of his friends teased him about his strict adherence to the cautionary guidelines of utilities, saying he was the only managing director of a multimillion-rand company who was this obedient to the authority of plumbers, electricians, pool services and the like. *Hey* – he'd object – *I like my life, and I want to teach my children to be careful.* Of course, there was only one child, Becky. People asked them when they planned to have another baby, and they'd smile at each other and reply – *we're practising.*

At the deep end corner where he'd not yet fastened the net, he eased his way between it and the edge of the pool, into the water, his naked pale body disappearing by bits into the slimy darkness. His leg brushed up against something solid and moving. He froze, then carried on preparing himself. It was only the pipe of the Hug Bug. Hug Bug the Whale.

This was going to be the hard part. He reached over his shoulder for the remaining unfastened hooks, and straightened the webbing as best he could. Then he began to fasten the hooks. He had to stretch his arm over the terracotta lip of the pool. There were three black outer mid-section hooks on either side of the corner, and he managed these after some effort.

He started on the three red corner hooks, the only remaining ones. It was awkward, hard work, especially as his feet didn't reach the bottom of the pool. He had to try to maintain a foothold, a lever for his body as he worked at the net, his feet scrambling for a grip along the slippery slope where the side curves to meet the bottom of the pool, as he pulled the rope with one hand to try to create enough slack for him to bring the hook in line with its eye, then past the edge of the eye and slot it into place. Finally, he got it in. The next was trickier, the grid having tightened even more. His fingers and hands ached, little cuts opening up, and then he slipped and his nail caught somewhere, ripping it away from the soft, vulnerable flesh beneath. He got the second red into its slot. All those sessions in the gym have helped, he thought. He was now firmly in the corner, the last hook to put in place. This was the corner where, three months before, he'd found Becky, her little body weighed down by her water-logged lungs.

He took a breath and prepared to tackle the last red. Someone would phone Janet at her parents' house and tell her that he'd finally put the net on, he who had always been so careful to follow safety instructions and had once, only once, not been so careful. He let go of the last red hook. It didn't seem to matter. The net stretched taut above his head. The day had gone. He stared past the blue bars of rope into the night sky. The water level was over the third mosaic now, and he had to tilt his head so that his nose was in the air, like a snorkel, and his ears under the green water, and he could hear the reassuring gurgle of Hug Bug the Whale coming up from the depths to greet him.

THE BEGGAR IN
THE BOOKSHOP

The day I fled the country I went to my father's bookshop in Commissioner Street, just up the road from John Vorster Square. He was sorting through a new consignment, and he looked up, alerted by the *bing-bong* of the electronic door chime.

'Robert, glad you came. Help me stack these will you? Here, that lot in antiquity, the others in the English lit section.'

I picked up one of the books he'd indicated. 'What about this one?' It was Douglas Bader's biography, *Reach for the Sky*.

'Ah, let's see. Humour?'

You had to know my father to understand the joke. It was a standing joke, so to speak. My father and his veteran buddies used to make fun of Bader, of the fuss the World War II flying ace made of being able to walk after he'd lost his legs. The joke was that, while he'd lost his right leg up to the thigh, he'd only lost the lower portion of his left. It was easy to walk if you still had one knee joint.

I was seven or eight when I first noticed, *really noticed*, that Dad was different. We were over at friends. The kids were in the water, along with a couple of the adults, and Dad decided to jump in. There were some people there who'd never met him before, and they stared when he appeared for his swim. He walked to the pool on his hands, his lower body – what was left of it – thrust forward for balance, the stumps of his thighs poking out of his shorts. Manipulating himself like a gymnast on a pommel horse, the muscles of his upper arms pumped, he brought himself to the water's edge, then lowered himself in. It was all deep end to him, a five-year-old stood taller than he did. Seeing him through the reticent eyes of those strangers, I thought, he's different, he's not like everybody else's dad. He has no legs.

We were stacking in adjacent rows, opposite each other, so that every now and then, over the shadowed edges of the books' spines, I caught sight of his face, on the tip of his nose the reading glasses that would hang on his chest whenever he didn't need them. His neatly combed black hair – slicked down with Brylcreem – the cropped pilot's moustache, thin lips. Those pale grey eyes. Before losing his legs, he would've been shorter than the height I'd grown to, but he'd had the prosthetics people add a few inches.

'I'm leaving tonight,' I said. It was 1985, the country festering under a State of Emergency.

'So, you're actually going, are you?'

'Yes. I don't have much choice, do I?'

'Crap, Robert. You have all the choice in the world. You can do what all the other boys are doing.'

Some of the other boys were going to university to avoid the army. But Dad wouldn't hear of that.

'Country first, yourself second,' he said.

I agreed with the sentiment, only this was apartheid South Africa. 'Country first' had people hacking one another with pangas or tossing detainees out of tenth floor windows.

We finished our piles, and I followed him to the front where the boxes of new books lay. His style of mobility required an effort which he almost masked by the rhythm he managed to inject into it. Without knee joints, with your prostheses strapped to your thigh stumps, you have only your hips to walk with, you must swing the entire leg apparatus from just that one joint. Douglas Bader's intact left knee gave him two joints to work with, leaving only the mechanical ankle of that leg to manipulate.

My dad walked by kicking each stump upward. The knee would bend automatically. Then he kicked the stump downward, landing on his foot. Without ankle and toe muscles to spring him off, he had to push his upper body over his legs, which he did by leaning forward, unbalancing himself so that his torso weight carried him over the leg that was placed in front, then using his momentum to keep walking. Kick the stump forward, then downward, like the cracking of a whip.

Dad had refused to use a walking stick at home or at work, where the evenness of the floor was predictable and there were surfaces to hold onto. Outside, a crack in the pavement could up-end him.

We got to the front as an old man on crutches came shuffling in through the door. 'I haven't eaten in two days, baas. Baas, I can't work, baas. Look here.' The beggar gestured to his stump. He was wearing someone's old army browns, grimy, knotted below the amputated thigh. 'Please, baas, only fifty cents for some bread.'

'What rot!' My father growled. 'Get a job! If I can work with no legs, you can work with one!' He snatched one of the beggar's crutches from him, leaving the old man wobbling in the doorway, and landed a smart blow against each of his own prostheses. Dad enjoyed the look on people's faces when something heavy came down on those legs. He used to do that when I'd displeased him as a kid. I'd be hovering just out of reach, and he'd pull his belt out of the loops of his pants and whack it against himself, just as his pants began to slip down, revealing his underpants and the elaborate set of straps and corsetry that fastened his legs to him.

In the bookshop that day, with the old man still teetering on his good leg, my father tossed the crutch back at him. It struck the doorframe and clattered to the ground. I picked it up, reached out to steady the old man, and helped him out of the shop.

'Here,' I said, giving him the coins in my pocket.

'Thank you, kleinbaas,' he said.

I watched him shifting away, the knot of trouser leg swinging to his slow shuffle.

'Don't pity them, boy! You do that and they'll never stand on their own two feet.'

'Two feet, very funny, Dad.'

'And what do I have? Three?'

'We've been educated, Dad. No training, no

education, all a Black man has is his labour. How do you manage that on crutches?'

'Rubbish! I get around this shop, don't I? Who the hell do you think packs all these books?'

I knew how chafed his thighs got. When I was younger, I'd watch him rub cream on them.

'In any case,' my father said, 'do you think he really means all that *baas* nonsense? Huh! He's working us. It's these stupid ideas of yours, Robert. This country's given you everything you've got. You're being a damn ingrate.'

'I—.' No point finishing my sentence, he'd already anticipated my rebuttal.

'Crap! We fought Hitler to keep this country free!' He slapped his legs. 'I've earned the right to give you what I have. And now you're kicking me in the teeth. Christ, I thought you'd come to your senses. Told your mother, even. You're my son after all, goddammit!' He shook his head. 'To think that a Fourie man would refuse to serve. You've brought shame on the family, Robert. I'm bloody ashamed of you!' I thought he was going to reach for his belt, but he just stood there shaking his head.

It was only later that the sting in his words made room for what I could have said: Dad, you taught me this. You taught me to stand up to bad men. You're famous for it. You're the one who flew Marylands on daylight raids on the harbour at Benghazi and then, in a plane so badly shot-up it should've fallen into the sea, managed to limp your way hundreds of miles through thick cloud with ice forming on the wings to a crash-landing at Sidi Barrani, bringing your crew safely home. Only you left your legs in the desert. And then, barely two weeks later, told General Smuts when he bent over to pin that medal to your chest, 'My friends were always on at me to lose some weight. So I did. Thirty-five pounds. All in the legs.' Guts and self-belief, that was you, taking the fight to the Axis fascists. How can you not see that our country's real enemy is its own government?

'Goodbye, Dad,' was all I could muster before walking out of the shop. I didn't want him to see a Fourie man crying. A seventeen-year-old Fourie man.

Later, Mom took me to the airport, reassuring me all the way that they wouldn't stop me at passport control, and that Dad would still talk to me.

'He'll calm down,' she said. 'It's just the shock of your leaving, that's all. He's going to miss you terribly, you know.'

'He has a funny way of showing it.'

'He just can't be soft, that's all. You mean everything to him.'

I took my seat on the plane, in my bag a little money she'd managed to save and the number of a conscientious objectors' group in London.

It was after the war – don't ask which one, as far as Dad was concerned there was only one war – after he'd learned to walk again, that he opened his bookshop. He'd had to move a few times. They kept tearing down the buildings. The last place he'd taken about twenty years ago. The stock piled up, the shelves buckled, the aisles increasingly littered with overflows of books waiting like literary landmines to trip up unsuspecting browsers. The stacks were so close together, if two people were there at once, one would have to retreat into the slightly broader main aisle for the other to get past. Occasionally he'd have to deal with a health inspector who he'd need to sweet-talk in order not to get the place condemned as a fire hazard.

After I left in 1985, my contact with him was limited to a footnote at the ends of my letters to Mom. In December 1989 I got my first letter from him. Mom had passed away. He'd already buried her.

'You weren't going to come anyway,' he wrote.

I did go back. In '97. We could finally afford a holiday. No, that's not the reason. A few years before, when it was safe for conscientious objectors to return, my wife said to me, 'Go! See your father. We'll be fine.'

'It's too expensive,' I told her. 'We can't afford it.' But we both knew it was an excuse. I couldn't go back. I wasn't ready. I'd have to face him without the comforting buffer of my mother. I'd have to face her awful absence.

When we got to Johannesburg, I left Felicity and the kids at the hotel and drove the hired car into town. I'd written to tell Dad I was coming. What if he hadn't got the letter? I should have phoned.

The streets had changed. On the way I passed a new Hyatt and a new Hilton. Vendors on the pavements, trellis tables loaded with leather goods, children's toys, African art. Posters on poles advertised an upcoming rugby test, the shows of an American dance company. Hawkers and beggars hovered at the windows of cars waiting for traffic lights to change. You could do your shopping from your car: clothes hangers, window shields, driver-friendly notebooks. A man in a clown outfit handed me a leaflet for a new townhouse development. *SECURE, SAFE SURROUNDINGS*, it read. At each light, open hands insistent at closed windows and blinkered faces. The playing fields were being levelled – here were white beggars. And then there were the ghostly thieves. Which ones were they? This tummy-rubbing child moving hungrily between the vehicles? Or that man with the misspelt plea on his piece of cardboard? I'd been warned. Keep your windows closed, doors locked. Don't leave any bags or valuables in sight.

In town I drove into a parking lot a couple of streets up from the shop and paid the attendant. Walking along I suddenly thought, what if he's moved again? Maybe they've torn the building down. And then, what if he's died and nobody told me. I didn't recognise many of the shops. I passed some vendors cooking boerewors and mielies on open drums, turned a corner and there was the familiar façade.

He sat reading, taking a moment to register that I had come into the shop. He looked up from his book, slipped his reading glasses off his nose. They dropped onto his chest.

'Hello, Dad.'

'Ah, so you've arrived, have you?'

'Yes. Got here this morning.'

'And your wife?' He looked behind me, toward the door. 'And the children?'

'They're at the hotel. Resting.'

'Yes, I suppose they must be tired. It's a long flight. How old are they now?'

'Marie's six and Damon's four.'

'Ah, yes, that's right. You named the girl after your mother. Marie would've liked that. I must take you to see her grave. You've not been there yet, have you?'

'No. I came straight here.'

'Good. We can go later. Her flowers need changing.'

'Flowers?'

'I take her flowers every week. Roses, usually. They were her favourites.'

'How,' I said, '– how've you been?' I stuck my hand out to shake his.

'Hell,' he said, pulling himself up. Chairs were another challenge for him. No knee joints to take the weight. Steadying himself on a nearby counter, or table, or armrest, he had to push with great force, and then make sure he didn't topple over. He took my hand and pulled me towards him. He'd never hugged me in his life.

I let go. 'You seem a little...'

'Shorter?' he said.

'Yes.'

'I am. Had the height adjusted. Makes it easier. Muscle strain, something in the back. I'm getting older.'

He'd re-arranged the shop. The counter had been moved to one side, up against the window, and in its place was an arrangement of two worn-out easy chairs and a coffee table with a packet of tea, a tin of Ricoffy, sugar, milk powder, and a kettle on a tray. He'd moved the stacks around too.

'I see you've moved War up here,' I said. 'Thought you always said you had to have something lighter in the front.'

'Doesn't matter now. No-one comes in anymore.'

'What do you mean, no-one?'

'Oh, one, maybe two people a week.'

'And you stay open for them? To sell one or two books a week?'

'Open at 8:00, close at 5:00. Been doing it for fifty years. I'm not about to stop now.'

He grabbed a walking stick that was leaning up against the chair he'd been sitting in and headed towards the back of the shop. Reaching the sink, he steadied himself on a nearby shelf, turned around, two coffee mugs in his hand, and made his way back to the front of the shop.

'What's this?' I was pointing to a clutch of objects –
small animal parts, feathers, a leather pouch – next to
the kettle on the coffee table.

'Good luck muti,' he said. 'To keep the place safe.'

'You were attacked?'

'No, of course not,' he laughed, switching the kettle
on. 'I've got the muti.'

I strolled down the aisles. At the back of the shop,
where the stacks for Law and Philosophy used to be,
was a metal bunk bed, neatly made-up. Next to the
bed, on a small table made from a set of *Encyclopaedia
Britannica*, was a reading lamp, and in the corner, a
heater.

'Dad!' I called out. 'Are you sleeping here? What
about the house? You've still got it haven't you? Dad?'

'Of course I've still got it,' he called back. 'The car,
too. You're talking about the bed? It's for an old army
comrade.'

'Oh,' I said, more to the rows of books separating
us than to him. I went back to the front and pointed at
the chairs. 'That's what these are for?'

'What? Oh, yes. More comfortable.'

'And that's why War's up here now?'

'Ja. Easier to get to when we're arguing a point.
Like this morning. We were talking about the numbers

of Black servicemen Up North. Native Military Corps, Cape Corps together. I said it couldn't have been more than a few thousand, he said more than fifteen... He was right.'

'*He* was right?'

'Yes. And you know what?' Dad began to laugh. 'He even has more leg joints than Douglas Bader. How do you like your coffee?'

'Milk, no sugar. Thanks.'

'Cremora okay for you?'

'Sure.'

The kettle was reaching boiling point. I wandered down the aisles again, looking for the children's section. I wanted to ask Dad if I could take some books back for the kids.

The door chime rang. What did he mean no-one came anymore? I hadn't been in the shop ten minutes and there was a customer.

'So, you've got them?' Dad's voice.

'Ja,' came a man's reply, 'they wanted thirteen rands. For two packets of biscuits!'

'Up North they cost nothing.'

'Yes,' said the man. 'But before Tripoli there were shortages.'

'Only for you lot.'

'Ja! That's true.'

I came from behind a stack to see the smile on Dad's face. 'Mandla,' he said to the man, 'this is Robert, my son. He's arrived.'

'Ah, the son! Robert, it is a long time your father and I have waited to see you again.'

'Do I know you?'

He came towards me, the yaw of an artificial limb in his step. 'What do you think?' He tapped his knuckles against his leg. 'No more crutches, *kleinbaas*.'

FUGUE

He was in a part of town he did not recognize. He'd lived in Johannesburg all his life but had never had reason to visit this area, or even drive through it. The small, post-war houses huddled behind low walls, weeds sprouting from cracks in the sidewalks and, despite the late hour, here and there, a muted light shone, the ghostly breath of uninhabited living rooms detectable through lace curtains. He'd been walking for hours.

He crossed the deserted road, stepping around a pothole poorly illuminated by the dim glow of the streetlights. He looked past the roofs of the houses, trying to find the Brixton Tower, sure it should have been to the south of his position. Perhaps it was obscured by the dark.

Kruger had decided to make his own way home.

He knew his friends and colleagues would think him absurd. Václav had given him a lift earlier in the evening but Kruger wasn't in the mood to risk it. At the best of times, the timpanist was a serial complainer, and the pitch of his grievances, when he was drunk, grated unbearably. Tonight, he was very drunk. They all had much more than usual to gripe about. The Orchestra's funding had dried up. They had played their last concert.

He came to a fork in the road and chose what he thought was the northern route. Christ. A visiting conductor once said of the grumbling members of the Orchestra, 'You sound just like the Berlin Philharmonic – until you start playing.' But no matter. They may not have been the Berlin Philharmonic, but when they played, they still made beautiful music. Kruger was going to miss it terribly.

In a grand gesture of defiance, the musicians voted to give a free farewell concert for their devoted audience. Some felt the audience hadn't been quite devoted enough to come up with the money that would sustain their vocation but the Orchestra cost millions every year and without corporate or government funding, how could one expect private individuals to carry the load?

At the restaurant after the farewell concert, Václav was not the only one to get drunk. Most of them did. The bassoonist, Jessica, who was known to eschew the use of underwear, danced on the tables, her long black concert skirt hitched up in bunches around her hips and thighs. On stage, in rehearsal or concert, she seemed to enjoy presenting a rather startling view of herself to the viola players, if they cared to turn around and glance to one or other side of the instrument that rested between her thighs. Now she'd given the other musicians a chance to see what they'd been missing.

The Orchestra's demise had come as a surprise, despite being heralded. Bankruptcy was an ever-present refrain, on the score sheet with such metronomic regularity everyone had grown unfazed. Or, more to the point, they had been fazed for so long they'd stopped hearing the beat of doom, and took the most recent omens to be, like the others before them, a false alarm.

Kruger could have left years before. The Orchestra, the country.

'We must go,' Anne would say over breakfast, in bed, everywhere. 'Before we start a family.' She wanted to go to Sydney, where her sister lived.

'What will I do in Australia? They've got their own

musicians to feed.'

'I'll get a job,' she'd say. 'You could teach.'

'I love playing in the Orchestra.'

'I'm scared,' she'd said. 'I don't want to raise children here.'

Perhaps he should have listened. On a few fronts.

Now, as he walked, he took solace in the fact that he was not a cellist, or worse, a bassist. He would never manage the walk home. His flute, snuggled in the soft red velvet insides of its black case in the haversack strapped to his back, weighed little.

In a varied program, they'd played Aaron Copland's *Appalachian Spring*, which never failed to make him cry. It took him, alone, to a hostile place, and then rescued him with the tender company of friends, and the singing of old, familiar songs. At the beginning of the concert, he'd picked up the flute with his habitual apprehension. Stupid, he told himself. To feel nervous. But whether he was rehearsing on his own or performing for hundreds of people, it was always the same, and today was no different. He loved the character of his flute, its rich, warm timbre, capable of such variation, the sound spreading to every nook of the concert hall. But every time he drew the instrument to his lips it met the question: would the flute love him back? Would it *give* to him? Would he feel the *buzz* under his fingers, the flute's vibration conducting itself, joining silver to flesh in bionic wizardry. Would it be a good day?

There was only so much of Jessica's private parts anyone could take.

'Just little bit longer,' slurred Václav, who seemed not to have had his fill of drink or Jessica's flashing, 'an' I'll drop you home. Snug as bug in rug.'

'No, thank you,' said Kruger. 'I need the fresh air. I'll walk.'

And he had slipped away. It was way past midnight and he had students in the morning, work he would now have to expand, even though his needs were few, especially now that Anne had left, taken up with a doctor, fallen pregnant, and gone to live in Sydney. All in the space of six months.

He was out of the residential area now, walking past a row of boutiques. An old white man, shoulders hunched, rummaged in a garbage can, and then straightened up. In his hands was a pineapple. He held it up, fingers prodding at the thick spiky skin. He was feeling to see how ripe it was, as if he was a discerning shopper in a fruit and vegetable store. Nearing the old man, in the light cast from one of the shop windows, Kruger could see the long, scraggly hair was a washed-out blonde, the bleached hair of a surfer. The man wasn't that old after all.

Kruger didn't think he would be scrounging in garbage cans; he was not unduly concerned about his financial situation. Or not, at least, as worried as Václav and the others who had families to support. The only other living thing in Kruger's cottage was Sushi, his goldfish. Sushi's expenses were not high.

More than the Copland, Kruger loved the last piece of the evening, Bach's *Suite in B Minor* for flute and strings, planned, and played, in anticipation of the audience wanting more at the end of the scheduled programme. He was thrilled at its inclusion, not because he would be featured but because he believed that there would be no music as we know it without that village organist, Bach. What a mathematical genius! Kruger himself did not think on that side of his brain, and never tried to remember a sequence of notes. He only tried to imagine the sound of it.

He should not have been standing in front of the orchestra. Bach, he believed, had not conceived of his second *Suite* as a concerto. The flute should sit in the body of the orchestra. If you stand out in front, people expect more from you. They are waiting to hear a solo, and they get, for the most part, the flute playing in unison with the orchestra.

But there it was, Bach bastardized. And so, he stood near the conductor's podium, and played along with the grand, processional opening, the French overture in dotted rhythm. And then, for a moment, rested, the instrument poised in his hands. Metal and intimacy. Anne never understood how he could love a machine so deeply. But it was *his* machine. It was his saliva on the gold mouthpiece, his fingers impressing life upon the silver keys, his DNA in the flute's patina. The metal had taken in his touch. Anne never really did that. She wanted a partner, not a musician.

His moment came in the middle of the Bach overture: the fugue. He pressed his lower lip to the flute and breathed, and blew, his fingers dancing across the keys, the notes flying with Bach's idea. He had been so frightened that he would crack a note. And then he did. The tears had choked his voice. At least, he thought, it was not Mozart, not that perfect, unforgiving god. But still, he felt wretched. He had cracked a note. He had done violence to the music.

At the end of the *Suite*, he'd been unable to hear the applause of the audience, unable to see them on their feet, their silent hands moving together in a mimed clap. Had they not heard the cracked note?

The conductor nudged him to take a bow, took him by the hand off the stage, and then led him back to take another bow, and another.

It seemed almost a different town, perhaps even a different country. He tried to identify the cars, few that there were. They drove on the left-hand side of the road. That was right. Was that a Toyota? A Mazda? The dawn sky was becoming clear, a very pale blue. There was something about the air. And the humidity.

A brace of sex shops to his left. He didn't recall seeing them before. He should tell Václav about them. He was walking towards tall office blocks. There was a park. Perhaps if he walked through it, the trees and waking birds would bring clarity to his mind. He crossed a road, to another section of the park. It was light now, daytime. He came to the end of the park. Broad and black, like some dark tongue, a road stretched out in front of him. The blue-black tongue of a chow. He smelled his dog's breath armpits. It was the smell of a man who had not bathed in days. The restaurants here were unfamiliar, the high rises surely far too substantial for him not to know them. He was coming down an incline, startled by a train thundering by, the road sloping down towards an expanse of blue. He gaped. Had the sky inverted itself? Was this a trick of the early morning light? A bank of blue fog? How could this be? He'd been walking through the streets of Johannesburg after the Orchestra's last concert and the drunken farewell at the restaurant, walking through streets unfamiliar though they were, but now to come over a rise and be confronted by… a harbour?

He kept going, drawn by the blue, now framed beneath a snaking concrete path. Another train, on a monorail. Since when did Johannesburg have a monorail? And ferries leaving a wharf? And then… the sails of the… *Sydney Opera House?* He had seen postcards, documentaries. He'd always thought they resembled seashells rather than the sails of the architect's intention. Unlike Anne, though, he'd never actually seen them.

His flute case in hand, he shuffled towards the Opera House. Perhaps the road would melt beneath his feet, the buildings evaporate. He might fall. Cars hooted as he crossed roads. He brushed past people. It seemed to take an age, as if the familiarity of the landmark should have made it closer to wherever he was. Finally, he arrived, and sat down on one of the steps of the forecourt. A ferry was moving by, schoolgirls pressed up against its side. He could see the fluid movement of their lips, their animated chatting, their voices lost across the water. He glanced over his shoulder, at the bridge. A row of people in overalls seemed to be working their way steadily up its arc. Perhaps they were a club of suicides, he thought. These cults were doing it all the time. And this was a beautiful place to die.

He wasn't sure what to do. What was going to happen to Sushi? Who was going to feed her? He took off the haversack and pulled out the black case that housed the flute. He felt the click of the catches. He opened the case and stroked the red velvet. The flute lay waiting for him. He picked up the head joint and pushed it into the socket, listening for the soft *chuck!* He turned the head to align it, then slid the foot joint home.

For a long while he sat looking at it. A group of tourists were taking pictures of the famous building behind him. He blew down the shaft to warm the flute and then brought the instrument to his mouth. Would it love him back? Would it give to him? Would he feel the buzz?

He played the solo part from the fugue in the *Suite in B Minor*, began the motif, went on for a few bars, flying away with the music, then listened for the other instruments as they came in one by one, each flying away in turn, now this voice in imitative counterpoint, now that one, in a different pitch, and another, and another, the voices working independently, yet linearly, articulating and winding about one another like the plaited columns of a noble edifice. His colleagues were sitting behind him on their chairs, music open on the stands in front of them, the conductor's baton pointing and prancing, the dark audience silent. The music was architecture reproducing itself. He was playing with the Berlin Philharmonic on the steps of the Sydney Opera House. He could feel the *buzz*.

And then each voice returned from its flight and came together like the protean pitches of the roof behind him. Dancing together. Coupling. The tears that fell from his eyes were caught by his unshaven cheeks.

A woman came up to him, fiddling in her handbag. She took out a purse, her long fingers exploring its insides, removed a coin and dropped it into the flute case that lay open at his feet. Kruger, the former Principal Flautist of the South African National Symphony Orchestra, raised his eyes. A small crowd had gathered in a semi-circle around him.

The fugue at an end, without taking his fingers from the keys, Kruger lowered his instrument and watched as more coins came floating out of the crowd in an arc from the outstretched hands of the tourists, as if down the scalloped sails of the Opera House, landing with a *clink!* in the red velvet mouth of the waiting flute case.

GOLEM HEIGHTS

On Monday I saw her again. She was in her school uniform, walking along Kotze Street amongst its Black inhabitants, satchel on her back, thumbs hooked under the straps, Bafana Bafana beanie low over her ears and neck, a briar of auburn hair escaping its rim. A pale figure incongruous to the hustling streets of Hillbrow.

At Highpoint I waited for the lights to change, then lost sight of her. She must have turned down Twist. I've seen her a handful of times, around five when I come to collect Nomvula from work. Today, though, it was just past one. Why wasn't she still in school? When I first saw her, I thought she may be an albino child, so ashen was her skin, like stretched parchment. She can't be more than seven or eight, and she must be the only white child within a pistol shot of here.

'You're worried for her?' Nomvula laughed after I'd mentioned her a couple of weeks ago. 'She's umlungu so you think she's a target. Why more a target than any other kid?'

Nomvula was wrong, or at least, not quite right. I was worried but not because she was white. This girl moved about the streets like a ray through water, as if her environment was a placental sac of immunity, as if everyone was her friend. Her naiveté, it seemed to me, not her pale skin, made her a target. Sitting in my battered old Toyota waiting for Nomvula to emerge from the bank, I've watched the girl drift through the throng of hawkers, street kids, labourers, refugees, drug dealers, sex workers, her thumbs in their fixed positions under her satchel straps, now and then stopping to chat to a man selling brooms, a bewigged woman slouched against a doorframe, some kids kicking rolled-up rags along the pavement. Maybe they all sensed her like I did, the static electricity of her otherworldliness, as if she were a visiting royal, Princess Di chatting with the locals, shaking hands with AIDS patients or walking through a cleared minefield.

I stopped to buy a pack of Stuyvesants from the café, thoughts of the girl gone, my mind returning to the matter at hand, an interview I'd just set up with an old man on the hospital side of Hillbrow. Before I was back in the driver's seat, I'd dragged half the ciggie into my lungs. Glorious relief. I've always had a hard time sorting excitement from anxiety, and today was no different. My three-ciggie-a-day rule was heading for a bust. I'd first become aware of the old man's existence that very morning. Oddly, since it was but a few hours' earlier, I couldn't recall how he'd come to my attention, nor how I'd found his phone number. But I *had* to speak to him. He was something far more precious than all the papers and books and films I'd researched. He was *there*. An actor in some of the great German films of the silent era. He had to be ancient. God, the last silent film was made almost seventy years ago. Finding him was a spectacular coup; it was going to make my PhD. I stubbed the stompie into the car's ashtray.

I should know the suburb well. I grew up in nearby Yeoville. But when I turned into Kapteijn Street and drove up to his building and parked in front of its big glass doors, the Toyota mirrored there as if two of us had arrived – the one in the glass doors looking a lot smarter, the dings and patchy bodywork with its scattered rivulets of rust smoothed out by the glass darkened by the sombre interior behind it – the place looked unfamiliar. It was a trick of adaptation. If my childhood self had bolted forward to this time, I would not have recognised the entire Hillbrow precinct, so much has changed. But the old man's building, I realised, now felt unfamiliar because it *hadn't* changed.

Like many buildings in the suburb, this one was art deco. But not for this place the Lebensraum-grab of closed-in balconies, the graffitied brickwork and grimy, blistered plaster, the washing hanging limp from windows. The building was aging gracefully, the maintenance immaculate, the façade unadorned by the desperate overflow of people's lives. It was as if the place had forgotten to fall apart, a healthy member of a set of necrotic teeth.

As I reached for the heavy glass and brass-plated foyer door, it swung open. The notebook and Sony tape-recorder pinned under my arm almost fell. An old white man held the door ajar, his liver-spotted hand gripping the inside handle. Inclining a head that appeared far too large for the thin, tall body upon which it was perched, he beckoned me inside. I must have hesitated because he added, 'Come in, young lady.'

It seemed more an order than an invitation. I stepped inside, adjusting to the gloom of a vast space only dimly lit by recessed lighting high above. It is an unfortunate human habit that our eyes are drawn to imperfections. Or perhaps it is not human but animal, after all, a sizing up of a stranger, taking the measure of his wounds. The old man towered above me, the weight of his head leaning in towards mine, and my eyes mesmerised by the divots in his cheeks and on his chin, as if the flesh had been gouged out decades ago by terrible acne or the knife of an assailant. His eyes were hidden in the shadow of the black, shiny peak of a gold-braided cap, part of, I could now see, as I dragged my eyes from his scarred face, his doorman's uniform. The uniform had a faint patina, the hint of glory departed, of elegant decline not unlike the building he attended. He reminded me of the protagonist in *The Last Laugh* (1924), an old man who is ostracised by his friends and family after losing his prized job as doorman at a hotel. FW Murnau tells the story beautifully, without the use of subtitles.

The Doorman closed the door, or rather, he allowed the door to swing back under its own impressive weight. 'Can I help you, Miss?'

His accent was a layered cake, East European overlaid by other influences I could not distinguish. Like the gold braid on the chest front and sleeves of his dark blue uniform, and the golden tassels hanging from each sleeve cuff, ornamental accents that jarred against the claim Africa had made on Hillbrow.

Finally finding some words, I said, 'I've come to see Mr Herbert Neumann.'

'Ah,' he said. 'Yes, of course.'

He seemed to be mulling over his options. I gazed about the foyer, its vault swooping high overhead, supporting ribs resting on massive buttresses that ranged around the room – for that is what it was, a grand room, a fabulous Gothic space, empty apart from a row of four large terracotta pots, not unlike the Shona pot that sits in the corner of our lounge, mine and Nomvula's – how I would love her to see this place – only these pots stood shoulder height to the rangy doorman, cut strelitzias bursting from their clay innards, birds-of-paradise with the blue tongues of their flowers wagging out of orange mouths – and a black striated board with the names of the tenants spelled in white plastic lettering – not encased in glass on the wall, but supported on an easel, like those found in hotels directing visitors to a wedding. This board read like a slice of our new Rainbow Nation: Ndlovu, Levin, Sekgobe, Raphiri, Wolfson… Neumann. No numbers, just names. But what surprised me more than the absence of numbers was the presence of so many Jews still living here, perhaps the last outpost in a suburb where their brethren – my parents included – had fled to the leafier worlds of Houghton and Sandton.

The Doorman was looking at me patiently.

'Mr Neumann, 9F,' I offered, 'I have an appointment to see him. Miriam Gotkin.'

The old man coughed politely. 'Ah, yes, of course. You are Miss Miriam Gotkin,' he said, as if it was I who needed my identity confirmed. 'You are expected.'

'Oh… good.'

The Doorman's gaze seemed to say that he found me as strange a curiosity as I found him in his antiquated uniform, in this cavernous room late twentieth century Hillbrow, in this fifth year of South African democracy.

'You will find him on the ninth floor.' He hobbled over to the lift and pressed the UP button. The gold braid twined like plant tendrils along the bottom border of his jacket. He was looking at me, at my jeans and T-shirt and Doc Martens from the Oriental Plaza. He seemed to be having second thoughts about his decision to let me in.

'I guess I'm underdressed,' I said. 'I'm sorry. I heard

about him this morning. I got here as fast as I could.' I don't know why I was apologising. I suppose I was petrified he was going to change his mind and throw me out. 'I'm a PhD student,' I added by way of inane explanation, shrugging my shoulders in a you-know-how-poor-we-are kind of way. My gaze was on the floor, which had the gleam of polished dung. The word supplicant came to mind.

He smiled knowingly, although what exactly he knew was beyond me. I looked away, following the path of the lift. The brownish-yellow lights behind the cut-out numbers in their shiny brass plate crept down like insects trapped in amber from the top floor, which was the ninth, Mr Neumann's. The gogga on the fifth was illuminated when a side door opened. The Doorman twirled with surprising speed towards the disturbance. A man was in the doorway, behind him darkness. He loosened his grip on the door. Before it swung closed, I made out the gloomy shapes of cars and grimy pillars and the oil-spattered cement floor of a parking garage. The doorman, recouping his slowness, raised a hand in greeting.

'Good evening, Mr Mguni.'

'How goes it, Baba?'

'Very well, thank you. And yourself, sir?'

'I'm well. Need a tip for Saturday, Swallows vs. Chiefs. What d'ya think?' Mr Mguni winked at me.

'Swallows by two goals to one, I believe.'

'No kidding? Thanks! The usual percentage?'

The Doorman opened the door to the lift and then the ornate gates, which slid back with the velvety swish of curtains. Mr Mguni ushered me in and waved goodbye to the old man.

'The young lady's going to 9F,' the doorman called out as the door of the lift closed, its hinges sighing pleasantly.

'9F, uh?' said Mr Mguni.

'Yes.'

'You're going to see the old Jew, Mr Neumann?'

'Yes.' Discrete lighting in the lift. Walnut panelling. The wood and brass handle below the black Bakelite buttons. Above the door, an arrow began to traverse its crenulated half-moon of floor-numbers. No mirrors to relieve the closeness of the space, only the smooth ride up the shaft's mechanical throat.

'With him living in this building we don't have to put our beds on bricks anymore.' Mr Mguni chuckled, as if he were laughing at himself as well as the old man on the top floor.

'Is he alright? I mean, in his mind?'

'Oh, he's only a little mad, but we don't mind him. The grandchild helps him. The old woman on the eighth floor, she is another thing. She comes down, she'll stand there in the corner of the lift, leaning on her walking stick and she'll say to your face, "hey, darkie, where's my teaspoon? You took my teaspoon." She is mad, man. What would I want with her teaspoon? We just laugh.' He paused. I looked at the floor indicator. We were on four. The brass fittings in the lift reflected a muted brilliance, the work, I guessed, of the Doorman's Brasso-soaked rag.

'That old woman, her husband sold skin-lightening cream. Left her with a spare room full of the stuff. So she gives us one every Christmas.'

'Oh, shit,' I said. 'She's got no clue, has she?'

'No.'

'What do you do? When she gives you the jar of cream?'

'We thank her,' he smiled wistfully. 'And dump the cream in the rubbish.'

Mr Mguni smiled at me. 'There're lots of old Jews in this building.'

Nine. No jolt of arrival. I wasn't sure that the lift had stopped but he slid the grate back and pushed the door open. I got out and held it ajar.

'Oh, no, I'll be going back down. I'm on seven.' He smiled and waved, adding before the door closed: 'You know what they call this building? Indlu ka-Israyeli.'

Indlu ka-Israyeli, an easy test for a whitey who, like me, was raised by an African mama, with a lover whose first language is isiZulu. *The House of Israel.*

The corridor, open to one side, looked out over the southern rooftops of Hillbrow. I could make out urban fields of garbage cans and mosaics of washing poking out of windows or lying casually over cramped balcony walls. 9B's door was ajar, the security gate open. The only thing guarding the entrance was the mezuzah on the doorpost. I caught a glimpse of an elderly woman watching television. Lace curtains on kitchen and bathroom windows, tsatske in the window: pottery birds, a small basket of dried flowers, a glass salt and pepper set, a plastic container of Handy Andy. The kitchen door.

I went back. 'Excuse me, hello!'

'Oh, hello.' She waved.

'Sorry. Just wanted to tell you, your gate's open.'

'Oh, that's alright, dear. Thank you.'

Two doors down, a familiar smell. 9D was cooking something that took me back to my grandmother's kitchen in Welkom. I stopped for a moment to breathe it in. Kneidlach. Of course, I'd forgotten, Pesach was coming up, a story of liberation. Bobba would've been fretting away, removing ingredients from cupboards and jars, off shelves, pouring, stirring, tasting, all the while slapping our greedy little fingers away from her mixing bowls, miniature Cossacks come to raid her feast.

I saw the girl as I was coming up to 9F, the last flat on the floor. She was sitting in the shadow of the stairwell with a cardboard box on her lap, her pale, spindly legs illuminated by the sun, her schoolgirl's knees reddened by a recent scraping. The Bafana Bafana hat was still on her head, the auburn hair cascading over her shoulders. I couldn't see her satchel. She must've put it inside already. The grandchild. I wondered how she'd beaten me here; I saw her turning into Twist Street, a good three blocks away. Perhaps it was my stop for cigarettes.

'Hello,' I said.

She smiled. 'Do you want to see my silkworms?'

'Sure,' I said.

She opened the lid of the cardboard box. Six or seven worms were moving in slow concert on a small heap of leaves, their cadaverous skin reflecting the colour of the fingers that reached in to caress them.

'They're beautiful,' I said.

'Yes.'

'What kind of leaves are those?'

'They're beetroot. They're going to spin purple cocoons.'

'Oh,' I laughed, 'I used to do that.'

'When they hatch,' she said wistfully, 'they will mate, and the females will lay eggs and die.'

'That is sad,' I said.

I must have misread her tone because she shook her head. 'No,' she said, 'that's just what they do.'

'Oh, yes, that's true. Do you live here?' I asked. 'In 9F?'

'Yes.'

'I've come to see Mr Neumann. Is he your grandfather?'

'He's my zeyde.'

'What's your name?'

'My name is Miriam.'

I felt a prick of girlish excitement. 'That's the same as me! I'm also Miriam!'

She was distracted, transfixed by a silkworm shuffling across the back of her hand. 'When you come next time,' she said, as if to the silkworm, 'I'll show you the cocoons.' She shook the silkworm onto a leaf, closed the lid of the box, got to her feet, and walked in through the open door to 9F.

Was I to follow her? She'd made no signal, or at least no signal I understood. My dilemma was resolved by the appearance of a stooped figure leaning heavily on a carved wooden cane moving slowly towards me.

'Ah, welcome Miss Gotkin, come in, come in,' he turned and, working his way down a corridor crammed with bookshelves and sepia photographs towards a dining and sitting area, finally arriving at the entrance to this room, turned once more to me. 'Come, sit. You don't have to stand on ceremony. I'm old, but I'm not royalty. Sit, sit! You want something to drink? Some tea?'

'Thank you, if it's not too much trouble.' I was still standing, the tape-recorder and notebook under my arm, my car keys and pen gripped in the hand of the other.

'Trouble? When you get a bullet in the kopf, that's trouble. Tea is no trouble. You take milk? And sugar?'

'Yes, milk, sweetener if you have, otherwise one sugar. Thanks.'

Mr Neumann looked as though he had once been a big man. Now he was bent in the shape of an 'r', his body reduced to a lower-case letter of the alphabet.

He shuffled slowly to the kitchen, giving me a chance to look around the lounge. There were only two easy chairs. No television. A small dining room table, one of those crocheted white tablecloths sold by women who sit on the pavement working away at them. More bookcases stacked to the brim, and where there was floor space alongside, piles of books stood in lines against one another, sometimes overlapping like the brickwork of a wall, each stack holding up the next. Most of the books looked very old, the mottled dull browns and blues of leather-binding. I crouched down. The titles of many had been lost to the light or the creasing of the books' spines but I could make out a few. *The Mystical Qabalah*. Leopold Zunz's *The Sufferings of the Jews During the Middle Ages* lay on top of one pile. Here and there the shiny cover of a more recent publication. *South African Jewry*. Paul Johnson's *A History of the Jews*.

Mr Neumann came back in, a tea tray shaking dangerously in his grip. I was paralysed. Should I move to help and risk insulting him? Or sit and risk being seen as uncaring? I opted for the former and in the event, he settled the tray and its contents safely on the dining table. He stood swaying there, his bamboo spine stiff as it rocked back and forth, as if he were davening, and for a moment I thought he might have been. His eyes were closed, his lips synching agitatedly, his body genuflecting. I sat down in one of the easy chairs.

'Ah,' the old man turned keen eyes toward me, and as if he'd read my mind, 'you know about the old rabbi in Potchefstroom? When he was davening he used to rock so much on the heels of his feet that someone was always put behind him in case – and it did happen – he'd swing too far back and fall like a rotten tree to the floor, cracking his head on the side of the bimah. Ha!' He busied himself pouring the tea. 'You enjoy reading?'

'Reading, yes,' I replied, 'second only to movies.'

'Yes, yes. That is why you are here, because you are studying the old movies. Here, your tea.' He proffered the tea in hands that were, under the less onerous task of holding a teacup rather than a laden tray, steady enough. His face was almost level with mine as his bent-over shape stood in front of me. He had brought a plate of biscuits, Checkers specials, but seemed to forget to offer them.

'You have a very pretty granddaughter,' I said.

'Great-granddaughter,' he corrected. 'Her mother… a beautiful woman.'

'She doesn't live with you?'

He lowered himself into the other easy chair and was quiet for a while before he said what his quietness had told me. 'She does not live.'

'Oh, I'm so sorry.'

'But it is my childhood you want to know?'

'Yes, I was hoping you might talk to me about your experience of working in silent films. Your recollections of what it was like to work during that era?' Nomvula considers the title of my thesis too pretentious, even for a doctorate. *German Silent Film and the Treaty of Versailles: Art, Propaganda and the Vengeance of the Fallen.*

'Work?' Mr Neumann said. His face was broad, liver-spotted and puffy, framed by a mane of unruly white hair. He looked a bit like a mangy old lion. 'Yes, I suppose it was work.' He was lifting and dropping his open hand onto the arm of his chair, as if some part of his body needed to keep swaying.

'Do you mind if I turn my tape-recorder on? It will save me having to write down what you say. I mean, as you talk… to keep up, you know. I'll be writing everything down later.'

'Tape-recorder? Mmmm… You would like a biscuit? Help yourself.'

I lifted the Sony up in my hand. He seemed not to object, and so I turned it on. 'Would you tell me about those times? What it was like on set, what the directors and actors were like? I'm interested in the atmosphere of those early studios.'

'I was only a boy, you must know. Just a boy. Have a biscuit, please, Miss Gotkin. So you like reading...'

'But you had a fairly big part in *The Student of Prague*. You're given a credit. Amongst several other films.'

'Ah, but that was later, yes. But not that late. Hitler was just a failed revolutionary then. *The Student of Prague*. It was the first time they printed my name. Lots of sword fights.'

Fencing, you mean. The words almost escaped my lips. *The Student of Prague* involved fencing. Instead, I asked, 'How did you get started? What was your first film?'

'Please, Miss Gotkin, have a biscuit.'

'Thank you, I'm fine, really. To be honest, Mr Neumann, I'm so excited to talk to you, I can't eat a thing.'

He smiled.

'Your first film?'

'Oh, it was nothing. One afternoon, maybe. Very

small part.'

'It was called?'

He was searching my face. 'You must know, Miss Gotkin, as a student of these films, that one was a very, very anti-Semitic film.'

'Oh!' I nodded vigorously. He seemed embarrassed. It could mean only one film. 'You mean, *Der Golem*?'

'But how was I to know that at the time? How could anyone see it? We would be told to walk here, run there, open our mouths and eyes like so, do this or that. They were bits and pieces. Who could see the whole? I was only a boy. The director came to the marketplace to find his little actors.'

Der Golem (1920), Paul Wegener, Lyda Salmonova. A classic. Based on the Jewish myth of the Golem of Prague. A rabbi sculpts a giant clay statue and gives it life to help the troubled Jews of Prague. It eventually causes more trouble than good, but the rabbi has difficulty destroying it. The mannerisms and movement of *Der Golem* were later adopted by American movies in the horror genre, amongst them Boris Karloff's portrayal of the monster in *Frankenstein* (1931). It was, of course, central to my thesis of humiliation as the root of Germany's revenge upon the Jews.

'The recorder, it is on?'

'Yes. Is that okay?'

'I never made a talking film. Now I am talking!' He laughed. 'Where is that child? She would forget to eat if I didn't tell her.'

Mr Neumann's frown seemed to express some hesitation, but then he said gently, 'Miss Gotkin. You know of course where your name comes from?'

'My name?'

'Gotkin. *Gott* and *kind*. Godchild. Do you think you are a Godchild, Miss Gotkin?'

It was my turn to hesitate. 'I'm not sure I even believe in God, Mr Neumann. Actually, to be truthful, I don't.'

'Yes, yes. I see that now...' His open palm clapped down on the armrest.

He struggled to his feet. Had my admission of atheism ended the interview before it had really begun? My fear of having offended him was competing with the thought that I should put my tea down in case I'd need to catch him. But I was relieved on both counts. He steadied himself and then turned to me with a smile on his face. 'You know Yiddish?'

'A little.'

He was supporting his lop-sided weight on an

armrest of his chair. 'Chaim and Abie, they are sitting together in the lounge of an old age home,' he said. 'Chaim gets to his feet, very shaky. He's leaning on his walking stick, and he stops, like a wobbly statue, for two minutes – two minutes! Then slowly he moves, one slipper here, one slipper there, one in front of the other. Abie looks up at him and says, "Chaim, *avoohin loifstoo?*"' He laughed, his big, dilapidated lion face roaring softly and then, seeing my incomprehension, added, 'Where you running to?'

I laughed, but it was only much later that I realised the real gift of his joke. He had given me a beautiful example of the self-deprecating Jewish humour that has evolved in the face of loss and persecution. At the time, though, I was mesmerised by his mien, as if I was in an audience of 1890s movie-goers, staring wide-eyed at the magic on the silent screen.

He moved slowly over to a pile of books. For the first time I noticed the white yamulka on his head. I could've sworn it wasn't there when I came in but then perhaps it had simply blended in with his hair. It reminded me of the scene in *Der Golem* where the rabbi is shown praying without a head covering; instead of turning to God for help in bringing his golem to life, Rabbi Löw is depicted as a sorcerer beseeching Asmodeus, the prince of hell. The Prague legend has the rabbi inscribe the word *emét* – truth – on the forehead of the golem. Disabling his creation required the simple removal of the aleph – the first letter, and *emét* becomes *mét*, meaning death – and the golem would crumble to dust.

He returned to his chair where he backed himself in, falling with a dull plop into its waiting arms. In his hands was an old photograph album.

'You would like another biscuit? Can you see the child? She must have her medicine.'

'Shall I call her? Is she unwell?' I got up and walked to the front door and into the corridor outside, calling out for her. Miriam wasn't there. Was I supposed to look for her?

'She's not outside,' I said.

He was staring at the carpet, a worn Persian rug. 'No, no, my dear, I am sorry. I have it wrong. Sit, sit.'

I hovered. If the child needed her medicine, surely she should have it? I poked my head into the passage leading to the bedrooms and called out again. Nothing. Silence. A silent movie. I gave up.

'May I ask more about *Der Golem*? Do you remember anything else from that day? You said the director came to the marketplace?'

'It is better in this country,' he said.

I was beginning to wander about senility but the cataracts in his eyes, instead of dulling them, gave off the muted glare of bright lights shining through a blanket; this was not the decline of his brain so much as him declining to answer my questions. Did something need to be named first? After all, I was talking to an old Jewish man, raised in pre-World War II Germany.

'May I ask,' I said, 'when did you leave Germany?'

He thought a while. Again, I had the sense this was not a memory retrieval exercise, but rather a consideration of consent. Finally, he said, 'In 1947.'

My words came out with a dull thud. 'You were in the camps.'

He rolled up his sleeve and I stared at his tattoo. 'We were all in the camps here, Miss Gotkin.' He smiled apologetically, and closed his eyes, his leonine head bobbing rhythmically, until the pattern of his breathing shifted and settled into something gentle. He had fallen asleep. There was a noise outside of sirens. The old man carried on sleeping, the photograph album resting on his lap. I reached out for it, then retracted my hand.

I sat there a while, I don't know how long. Perhaps I,

too, fell asleep because suddenly the girl was tugging at my sleeve.

'Zeyde will sleep a long time. We are going away tomorrow but you can come back next week.'

I hadn't been able to get a clear idea from Miriam when they would be back, nor where they were going. She was as enigmatic as her great-grandfather. By Thursday, I could take the wait no longer. The phone rang unanswered. I called again on Friday.

Nomvula admonished me. 'The girl said *next* week.'

'Yes, but I can't wait.'

'You'll have to, lover,' she said, not unkindly.

By Sunday night I had made up my frantic mind: if my phone call went unanswered, I would go round to the deco building in Kapteijn Street. In bed that night I dreamed of golems, brought to life by a voice from hell. They were on the march across Europe, the earth trembling beneath their clay feet, echoing the scene from *Der Golem* in which the unleashing of the wandering Jews' anger is evoked. But in the metamorphosis of dreams, my marching golems became Emperor Qin Shi Huang's terracotta soldiers.

They, too, were marching across Europe. I woke terrified, clinging to Nomvula.

It is said that only the most pious of men can create a golem, and then only that the golem will not have the power of speech. To have given the power of speech to their creatures would have put the rabbis on a par with God. One set of instructions – there are many ways to make a golem, but this recipe belonged to a learned French rabbi – include a complicated set of incantations and 462 circuits you must dance, strictly in the right direction. It is said that the good Rabbi's disciples tried, danced the circuits in the wrong direction, and were found swallowed by the earth up to their navels, crying for help.

Mr Neumann did not answer his phone. Not when I called in the morning, nor every opportunity I had between a busy schedule of tutoring third years, a meeting with my PhD supervisor, and another with the other members of the organising committee for a forthcoming conference on the censoring of women's voices in film (I was to deliver a paper on Marilyn Monroe, arguing that she was not simply the victim of powerful men but rather of her own intelligence, too feminist to reconcile with her blonde bombshell persona). By late afternoon, I could handle it no longer and made my way to the university's parking lot and my beaten-up old Toyota. The light outside was darkening, the air pungent, a prelude to the thunderstorm that was about to burst. How fitting, no rain machine required, only my Nomvula, whose name, perhaps Mr Neumann might know, means mother of all rains.

The parking space in front of the great glass doors was empty again, and I pulled up, meeting the reflection of my car. As I walked towards the entrance, a trendy young Black couple came out, the man carrying an infant in his arms. I stepped aside to let them pass. Inside the cavernous foyer, made darker still by the storm-laden sky outside, I waited for my eyes to adjust, and for the Doorman to appear. I was determined to be composed in his inscrutable presence. Already his words were in my mind – *ah, yes, Miss Gotkin, you are expected* – or something to that effect forming on his lips, the carved face looming above me. *Ah, yes, Miss Gotkin*. Of course! Now I had it. I had the base notes of that cluttered accent. Czech. The base notes were Czech.

But surprise me he did. By his absence. Nowhere in the foyer could I make out the gangly figure of the Doorman. I walked past the board with the names of the old Jewish men and women and the younger Black couples and families of the building, still expecting him to materialise. I felt, with a moment's panic, for the notepad tucked under my arm. Despite the Doorman's absence, the foyer didn't feel empty. Something was crunching underfoot, as if children had brought sand from the beach into the building. But of course, the nearest beach was hundreds of kilometres away.

I moved quickly towards the lift. I wanted to enter that ark, hear the soft swish of the gate, ride it to the ninth floor, be greeted by Miriam with her box on her lap, of what would now be, a week later, purple cocoons, welcomed by Mr Neumann at the doorstep to 9F, thank him with effusive relief and apologies for troubling him without an appointment, and to hear him say, *trouble? A bullet in the kopf, that's trouble.*

On the ninth floor, nothing. To one side, the row of kitchens and front doors and bathroom windows in shadow, to the other, the disorder of the suburb buttered over by a ray of sunlight breaking through the storm-freighted sky. The door to the old woman in 9B with the lace curtains and tsatske in the window was closed, along with the security gate. The tsatske were gone. No auburn-haired pale girl sitting in the stairwell just past 9F, the door to Mr Neumann's flat closed. I knocked. Once. Twice. Again. I tried the handle. Locked. I peeked in through the kitchen window. A glimpse of the bookshelves in the hallway. What was there to do? I hammered on the door with the palm of my hand. It came away reddened, like Miriam's knees when I'd last seen them. I walked back to the lift.

Two of the block's Jewish contingent were waiting in front of the lift door. I stood with them, listening for the churning of the lift's motor. The old men were deep in conversation, each with a battered, ancient leather suitcase resting alongside on the tiled floor of the corridor, waiting for their carriage. Mr Neumann's words hurtled into my head: *We were all in the camps here, Miss Gotkin.*

'Nu, do you know what my clever great-granddaughter says to me?' the taller of the two old men asked his companion.

'Which great-granddaughter?' said the other. He cradled a small clay flowerpot in the crook of an arm, the pungent smell of a bedraggled narcissus wafting off it, mingling with my distress. My own grandfather, several years my grandmother's senior, spoke with the same accent as these two men. Lithuanian, like most of the original Jews of South Africa.

The lift arrived. In what looked like a rehearsed, choreographed movement, both men leant over and picked up their suitcase, the taller man opened the door, the other pushed the gates back. I felt as though I'd intruded upon a scene being shot, an extra not knowing her lines or her place, as I slipped inside before the gates could curtain back into place.

'Sophie, Debbie's child,' the taller man said. They were both staring at the brass plate with its brownish-yellow lights indicating our descent past the floors of the old deco building. 'I'm sitting on the back seat, she's sitting there right next to me, and I'm asking her, who lives in an igloo? "Eskimos", she says. Nu, that's my clever maideleh. "Wigwam!" I say. "Indians!" she says. And then we are driving along near her house – there in the north – and I say, "Caravans!" I'm thinking my clever little great-granddaughter will tell me, "Gypsies!" but what does she say? *"Security men!"* she says.' He shook his head. 'Ha! Is this a place to bring up young children? You should come and live in Hillbrow, I told my little Sophie, although I was really telling her mother – you should come here, like the Neumann child, there are no security caravans here.'

At this, both men lapsed into a laden silence. We were passing the fifth floor when the old man with the pot plant shook his head sadly, 'Now that all is changed.'

'Such a sadness,' said the other.

'And so pretty.'

'To take one so young.'

'God's will.'

'God?' exclaimed the taller man. 'What kind of god takes a child?'

His companion shifted the flowerpot to his other arm, the white flowers of the narcissus, some a crispy brown around the edges, shuddering with the movement. 'The god of cancer,' he said.

I felt like throwing up.

'And now we must all live with the security caravans,' he added.

'Who was it you wanted to see here, young lady?' asked the taller man, his eyes still raised toward the lift's floor indicator, and when I did not answer – could not answer – he repeated, 'Young lady?'

My mouth was dry, the words sticky on my tongue. 'Mr Neumann,' I rasped.

'Ach,' said the man with the pot plant, 'You are saying, Rabbi Neumann?'

'Wha—.' Why are the words from a surprised mind always interrogative adverbs? What? Why? How? I managed to add: 'Rabbi? Mr Neumann is a rabbi?'

'Yes, of course, a rabbi. A very learned one, young lady.'

Why does everyone here call me *young lady*? I'm thirty-five, for god's sake.

'You are brave to come here at night,' the other said. I'm sure he meant to say foolish. Not brave, *foolish*. That's what Nomvula had said. 'Let me at least come with you,' she'd said. 'Dark Nomvula will protect you.' As if being Black was any protection, I threw back at her, remembering her admonishment about the girls of Hillbrow.

'I couldn't wait,' I said. 'Besides, it's not night-time yet.' Technicality, Miriam. It would have been night if I had stayed. If Mr Neumann – *Rabbi* Neumann – had let me in. Had been there to let me in.

The lift came to a halt on the ground floor. The taller man opened the gates, picked up his suitcase and pushed the door open with his shoulder, for the first time making eye contact with me, his head inclined towards the foyer, a grim smile on his face. I got out, followed by the other old Holocaust survivor, the three of us almost clattering into Mr Mguni as he emerged from the door leading to the garage.

With a polite nod of his head, Mr Mguni greeted

the old men as they made their way across the foyer floor.

'Wait,' I called after them. 'I—'

'They have poor hearing,' Mr Mguni said. 'Can I help?'

'The girl… and her great-grandfather, Rabbi Neumann…'

'They are late,' he said gravely.

'Late?' I said, suddenly hopeful. 'They're still coming tonight?' I don't know what I was thinking. It's not like I don't know what a Black South African means when they say late.

'No. *Late*. Passed. The child died yesterday, and the old man, well, we found him here this morning. On the ground. One of the pots was broken, lots of clay, big pieces, small pieces, scattered all around him. He must have fallen against it. Cracked his skull.'

I should have accepted Nomvula's offer to come with me, my beautiful mother of the rains. I walked towards the door and the black name board, felt with panic, then relief, for the notepad tucked under my arm, and then remembered there was nothing in it. I had nothing, or at least, nothing I could use for my PhD. My Doc Martens crunched on the bits of clay left over from the clean-up that must have followed the discovery of Rabbi Neumann's body and the shattered pot. The other pots were there, four of them – how many had I seen the week before, was it not four? Shouldn't there now be three? – but what remained of the strelitzias that had burst from them seven days ago, orange sepals on fire, blue tongues pulsing with life, were now limp and sunken over the terracotta lips of the pots.

At the foot of the black name board was a big chunk of the broken pot the cleaners must have missed. I stooped to look at it. What I thought was the rough inside of the piece, since it was so deeply furrowed, was convex, and in the dim light looked like a Greek base-relief sculpture depicting the part of a face, the lips and scarred cheeks, the hollow of an eye socket and a fragment of the forehead, of the old Czech Doorman.

About the Author

Graeme Friedman's writing has been short-listed for the Commonwealth Writers' Prize (Africa best first book) and the M-Net Literary Award, and long-listed for the Sunday Times (SA) Fiction Prize and the Voss Literary Prize.

He has published the novels *The Fossil Artist* and *What the Boy Hears When the Girl Dreams*, and three works of non-fiction: *The Piano War*, a true story of love and survival during World War II; *Leaning Into Love*, a book about relationships co-authored with Joanne Fedler; and *Madiba's Boys*, which explores the history of apartheid through the biographies of two of South

Africa's most successful footballers, with a foreword by Nelson Mandela. His work has been translated into German, Danish, and Swedish.

Graeme was born and raised in Cape Town, South Africa. When he was nine years old, a Zimbabwean sangoma predicted a future career as a lawyer. The sangoma's scattered bones told a prescient tale: as a newly qualified clinical psychologist in the mid-1980s, Graeme's involvement in anti-apartheid mental health organisations led him into courtrooms around the country where he appeared as an expert witness for the defence in the political trials of freedom fighters. His passion for the intersection of law, politics and psychology has culminated in a PhD on the role of shame and storytelling in political violence and terrorism trials, a research interest which is ongoing.

Since 2001, Graeme has lived in Australia with his wife and children. For further information, please see www.graemefriedman.com.

www.ingramcontent.com/pod-product-compliance
Lightning Source LLC
Chambersburg PA
CBHW061442210726
48287CB00007B/2319